THE poet of *Beowulf* is unknown to us,        Anglo-Saxon, almost certainly a Christian, and perhaps a cleric. The main action of the poem is set in early sixth-century Scandinavia, and the earliest likely date for its composition is about 150 years later, the middle of the seventh century, when Christianity was beginning to spread throughout Anglo-Saxon England. Scholars now tend to place the poem's composition at some time in the late eighth or ninth century. The dating of the single manuscript in which the poem is found to the very beginning of the eleventh century provides us with the latest possible date for the poem. *Beowulf* is written in Old English, in the standard alliterative four-stress line common to all Anglo-Saxon poetry. The language of the original gives us little clue as to where in Anglo-Saxon England it was composed. Even though the poem bears some of the characteristics of oral composition—especially in its use of formulae—it seems likely that its composition was literary, though it was probably designed for oral recitation. There are no explicit references to Christianity, but there is a good deal of biblical allusion, especially to the Old Testament. The poem is also rich in allusions to the legendary world of Germanic heroism and Scandinavian history which we know mainly from Old Norse sources. Epic in length, style, and subject matter, *Beowulf* is also profoundly elegiac in tone, depicting a long-past world of monsters, heroes, and kings.

KEVIN CROSSLEY-HOLLAND is editor of *The Anglo-Saxon World* (Oxford World's Classics), translator of *The Exeter Book Riddles*, and author of *The Penguin Book of Norse Myths*. He has written seven volumes of poetry and is a Carnegie Medal-winning writer for children. He is a Fellow of the Royal Society of Literature.

HEATHER O'DONOGHUE is Vigfusson Rausing reader in Old Norse-Icelandic Literature in the University of Oxford, and a fellow of Linacre College. She is the author of *The Genesis of a Saga Narrative: Verse and Prose in Kormaks saga* (OUP) and works particularly on the links between Old Norse, Old English, and Irish literature.

## OXFORD WORLD'S CLASSICS

*For over 100 years Oxford World's Classics have brought
readers closer to the world's great literature. Now with over 700
titles—from the 4,000-year-old myths of Mesopotamia to the
twentieth century's greatest novels—the series makes available
lesser-known as well as celebrated writing.*

*The pocket-sized hardbacks of the early years contained
introductions by Virginia Woolf, T. S. Eliot, Graham Greene,
and other literary figures which enriched the experience of reading.
Today the series is recognized for its fine scholarship and
reliability in texts that span world literature, drama and poetry,
religion, philosophy and politics. Each edition includes perceptive
commentary and essential background information to meet the
changing needs of readers.*

OXFORD WORLD'S CLASSICS

# *Beowulf*
## *The Fight at Finnsburh*

*Translated by*
KEVIN CROSSLEY-HOLLAND

*Edited with an Introduction and Notes by*
HEATHER O'DONOGHUE

OXFORD
UNIVERSITY PRESS

# OXFORD
UNIVERSITY PRESS

Great Clarendon Street, Oxford OX2 6DP

Oxford University Press is a department of the University of Oxford.
It furthers the University's objective of excellence in research, scholarship,
and education by publishing worldwide in

Oxford New York

Athens Auckland Bangkok Bogotá Buenos Aires Calcutta
Cape Town Chennai Dar es Salaam Delhi Florence Hong Kong Istanbul
Karachi Kuala Lumpur Madrid Melbourne Mexico City Mumbai
Nairobi Paris São Paulo Singapore Taipei Tokyo Toronto Warsaw

with associated companies in Berlin Ibadan

Oxford is a registered trade mark of Oxford University Press
in the UK and in certain other countries

Published in the United States
by Oxford University Press Inc., New York

First published as an Oxford World's Classics paperback 1999
Reissued 2008

British Library Cataloguing in Publication Data

Data available

Library of Congress Cataloging in Publication Data
Beowulf. English
Beowulf; The fight at Finnsburh / translated by Kevin Crossley-
Holland; edited with an introduction by Heather O'Donoghue.
(Oxford world's classics)
1. English poetry—Old English, ca. 450–1100—Modernized versions.
2. Epic poetry, English (Old). I. Crossley-Holland, Kevin.
II. O'Donoghue, Heather. III. Fight at Finnesburg (Anglo-Saxon
poem). English. IV. Title. V. Series: Oxford world's classics
(Oxford University Press)
PR1583.C76 1999 829'.3—dc21 98–22104

ISBN 978-0-19-955529-1

19

Typeset by Graphicraft Limited, Hong Kong
Printed in Great Britain by
Clays Ltd, Elcograf S.p.A.

# CONTENTS

# INTRODUCTION

*Beowulf* is an Anglo-Saxon poem about Scandinavian characters and events in a half-legendary, half-historical Germanic past. Its length—over 3,000 lines—its subject matter—a hero fighting against the forces of evil in a world of vicious power struggles between tribes and kingdoms in early Northern Europe—and its abiding concerns—the dignity of human conduct and the value of heroic society—identify it at once as an epic poem, and specifically, heroic epic. Epic poetry has been described as 'an expression of a society's cultural heritage' and certainly, in its breadth of reference and the grandeur of its ethical conception, *Beowulf* has always been viewed as the defining text of the Anglo-Saxon world. But, in common with Homeric epic, *Beowulf* does not slot into any clear historical or social context. We do not know when or where in Anglo-Saxon England it was composed; whether it had an oral prehistory; what kind of author it had. We can only guess how its contemporaries regarded it, and who its audience might have been. Most tantalizingly, we do not know whether its picture of heroic life reflects reality, or literary tradition, or is the poet's own invention; some of the events and characters in the poem have their basis in historical fact, while others, including the monsters, and the hero Beowulf himself, belong to a wholly different order of reality, the mythic or legendary.

The poem tells the story of how its hero, Beowulf, gains renown by coming to the aid of Hrothgar, King of the Danes, killing first a terrifying humanoid monster, Grendel, and then the monster's infuriated, vengeful mother. Beowulf eventually becomes king of his own country, Geatland, but when he is old (as Hrothgar was when Beowulf came to kill Grendel) Geatland itself is threatened by a monster—a fiery dragon which Beowulf fights and kills, dying in the process. With the death of Beowulf comes another, different threat to the Geatish people: without their king, they will be vulnerable to attack from old enemies, and the poem ends with a lament for Beowulf which is also a lament for the future of the Geatish people and, by extension, an elegy for heroic society as a whole.

It is said to be characteristic of epic poetry that it explores and questions at the same time as it values and celebrates. Clearly, there is much to value in *Beowulf*: the courage and strength of the hero, his selflessness in journeying to Denmark to help Hrothgar, his success in leading his own people through a lifetime's security, and his last great deed, the killing of a mighty dragon. But there are uncomfortable questions, too. Is noble King Hrothgar a failure because he cannot prevail against Grendel? Was Beowulf foolhardy in the way he took on the dragon? And most insistently, what is the validity of the heroic ideal if its finest achievements are swiftly eclipsed by warfare, death, and darkness?

## Christian Influences

The material world of Hrothgar and Beowulf is lavishly affluent, from Heorot, the magnificent, towering hall of the Danes, to the decorated battle-gear and golden treasures exchanged as rewards for heroism or tokens of loyal esteem. In many ways, their ethical and social world is also elevated. The prevailing values are not simply those of a warrior society—courage, loyalty, and strength —admirable though they may be. Beowulf offers Hrothgar help in an exquisitely tactful, diplomatic way; Hrothgar welcomes him with dignified courtesy, and when he leaves, gives him sober and wise advice about the transience of fame and pays a moving tribute to all that Beowulf has done. It is hard to feel that the poet is doing anything other than celebrate the heroic past. But this enclave of propriety, civilized behaviour, and humane virtue is under threat not only from the monsters. Throughout the poem, Beowulf and Hrothgar are contrasted with treacherous, weak, or unpredictable rulers, and the histories of their own ruling houses are seen to be replete with betrayal, usurpation, and violence. And this evil is not a thing of the past. The Danes themselves are facing turmoil: Heorot is doomed to be burned to the ground after the failure of an attempted reconciliation with the Heathobards through the marriage of Hrothgar's daughter Freawaru to Ingeld, and the succession of Hrothgar's sons to the Danish throne may be under threat from Hrothgar's nephew, Hrothulf. In Geatland, although Beowulf, like Hrothulf, is the powerful nephew of a king with younger children, he remains impressively loyal to Hygelac's heirs after the king's death, even when offered the throne by Hygelac's queen. But after Beowulf's death, the resurgence of old feuds will result in a floodtide of violence against the Geats.

The *Beowulf* poet's re-creation of the Scandinavian past is thus richly ambivalent, and perhaps this reflects the poet's attitude towards his own Anglo-Saxon past, for he was undoubtedly a Christian—perhaps even a monk—even though the poem's concerns are secular, not religious, and set in a period which was pagan, as the poet and his audience would have known well. The authoritative voices of Anglo-Saxon Christianity were not at all inclined to tolerance of the pagan past. The most celebrated condemnation of any interest in the deeds and heroes of that past comes in a letter from the eighth-century churchman Alcuin, probably written to a Mercian bishop in 797, and it may be directly applicable to *Beowulf* itself, with its likely allusion to Ingeld, King of the Heathobards: 'Let the words of God be read during the meal of the clergy. There it is proper to listen to a lector, not a harp-player, to the work of the Church fathers, not the songs of the people. What has Ingeld got to do with Christ? The house is narrow; it cannot hold both. The King of Heaven wants nothing to do with so-called kings who are pagan and damned, for the eternal King reigns in Heaven; the damned pagan king laments in Hell.' But Alcuin's strongly worded protest testifies as much to the currency of heroic legend amongst Christians as to his own antipathy to it.

To judge from its secular literature, Anglo-Saxon culture was conservative and deeply rooted in the past. Genealogies of the kings of Wessex trace the royal line back to Woden, the chief of the old

Germanic gods, and in the *Anglo-Saxon Chronicle*, Scealdwa and Sceaf, names which clearly relate to Scyld Scefing, the legendary founder of the Danish royal house in *Beowulf*, are included amongst King Alfred's ancestors. Some clerics—perhaps those less rigorously orthodox than scholars such as Alcuin and Bede, and especially those with an aristocratic lineage—must still have valued the traditions of their ancestors, pre-Christian though they were, and it may be that there was recognition of the ancient kinship between Anglo-Saxons and Scandinavians.

There is no attempt by the *Beowulf* poet to elaborate on the paganism of his heroes, who are portrayed as righteous and pious characters, often invoking an Almighty God whose power, and relationship with mankind, are wholly compatible with Christian belief. Interestingly, such a figure is very different from what little we know of any of the Germanic pagan deities, who in any case operated as a pantheon. Only once does the poet reveal the Danes as the pagans they would actually have been; worn out by the terror of Grendel's attacks, they turn to the worship of heathen idols in their ignorance of the Lord. But there is no specific reference to Christianity or the New Testament in *Beowulf*; it seems that a sort of natural religion, compatible with Old Testament monotheism, offered the poet an edifying but neutral ethical territory in which his characters could be acceptably admirable to Christians without the obvious anachronism of explicit Christianity.

The poem is deeply imbued with both biblical material and Christian echoes, however. The minstrel in Heorot sings of Creation in biblical terms, and the Danes are presented as living in a little Eden before the arrival of Grendel. Grendel and his mother, whilst reminiscent of the monstrous walking dead of Old Norse tradition, share many features with the giants of the Old Testament apocrypha, and are explicitly stated to be the descendants of Cain, a progeny in a state of permanent feud with God. Beowulf is not only firmly aligned with the forces of good against evil, but also, as the saviour of the Danish people, cast as a Christ-like figure. These echoes are deepened as Beowulf confronts

Grendel's mother in an underwater lair the entrance to which recalls the mouth of Hell as described in Christian homilies, and it is at the ninth hour of the day—the time of Christ's death on the cross—that the waiting Danes give up hope that Beowulf will return alive.

## Composition and the Oral Tradition

That the poem evidently belongs to a Christian milieu does not help us to date it, and indeed the dating of *Beowulf* has been the subject of enduring scholarly controversy. According to Bede, the Angles, Saxons, and Jutes began to arrive in England from mainland Europe in the middle of the fifth century AD, and the coming of Christianity to Anglo-Saxon England is conventionally tied to St Augustine's mission to Kent in 597, although British Christians in the north and west of the country may have had some influence on their new Anglo-Saxon neighbours before this. But the poem could not in any case have belonged to this relatively brief period of insular Anglo-Saxon paganism. One of the key events in *Beowulf*—the death of Beowulf's lord, Hygelac—is recorded by the historian Gregory of Tours, and can be dated to the early decades of the sixth century. In the poem, Hygelac's death is followed by a period of disturbance in Geatland, and then by Beowulf's own fifty-year reign. Thus on these grounds alone *Beowulf* cannot possibly have come into being in its present form much earlier than the beginning of the seventh century. At the other extreme, the single surviving manuscript of the poem (British Library Cotton Vitellius A. xv) has been dated to the very beginning of the eleventh century. Since the Anglo-Saxon period stretches from the first coming of the Angles, Saxons, and Jutes in AD 449 to the Norman Conquest in 1066, possible dates for the poem's composition range from almost the beginning to almost the end of this whole era, though the fashion for dating the poem much later than the middle of the ninth century seems to have passed.

Some scholars have attempted to date *Beowulf* on historical grounds. The age of Bede, who lived from 673 to 735, or the decades following his death, once seemed to provide an ideal context for the poem: Christianity well established, Anglo-Saxon scholarship thriving, and, crucially, still some time before the onset of Viking raids, which were thought to have made a poem celebrating Scandinavian heroes unacceptable. But Anglo-Saxon England was never a fully unified entity, and was hardly ever more than a loose collection of individual kingdoms. If Anglo-Saxon clerics in Northumbria would not have welcomed *Beowulf* in the years following 793, when Viking raiders sacked the monastery at Lindisfarne, nevertheless, as Alcuin's letter shows, other parts of the country were certainly showing interest. There is little justification for disregarding the early ninth century simply because of Lindisfarne.

The prevalence of Viking attacks all over the British Isles throughout the later ninth century makes it hard to envisage an appreciative audience for *Beowulf* during this time, but sporadic raids turned to widespread settlement, and with it the possibility of a new sort of relationship between Anglo-Saxons and Scandinavians: an interest in shared origins rekindled by contact with their new Scandinavian neighbours. A second wave of Scandinavian attacks towards the end of the tenth century once seemed to mark the latest date for the poem's composition, but there has even been an attempt to show that the second of the poem's two scribes, working in the eleventh century, was the author (though the existence of some garbled word-forms in his text makes this suggestion highly unlikely).

The language of *Beowulf* has also been used in the attempt to date the poem. Some of the metrical features of the original, as well as the forms of the proper names, suggest that the poem is relatively early, but those keen to maintain the possibility of a late date argue that the poet might well have deliberately archaized the diction of his poetry—Old English poetry is notably conservative in its literary conventions anyway. Attempts to infer the poem's place of origin from its language face similar problems. Some word-forms are characteristic of the Anglian dialect of Old English, but this covered an enormous area of northern, central, and eastern England. In any case, any such forms may only be evidence of the regional identity of one of the poem's copyists; the alliterative, four-stress line of Anglo-Saxon poetry could accommodate a good many minor linguistic variations. *Beowulf* seems to resist being pinned down to any time or place more specific than Anglo-Saxon England.

It may also be too simplistic to view the poem as a written text which came into existence as an authorial product at some sharply defined moment in a particular place. Some scholars have preferred to regard *Beowulf* as a gradually evolving text, with its roots in short, oral heroic poems close in date to the historical events, and coalescing over centuries into the poem we now have. Early Germanic poetry would have been orally composed as well as recited before an audience, and the hallmarks of oral composition are evident in *Beowulf*. Chief among these is the formula—a standard phrase, or group of words, which can be repeated or varied while remaining the same in basic form or grammatical structure, and then applied in certain stock situations. Thus Beowulf may be described—more than once—as 'leader of the Geats' or one 'brave in battle'. These epithets can be varied: Hrothgar may be 'leader of the Danes', or Beowulf 'steadfast in warfare'. Such phrases recall the use of standard epithets in Homeric poetry—the wine-dark sea, or wide-ruling Agamemnon. Formulae are not simply repeated and varied within one poem; most are common throughout the whole corpus of Anglo-Saxon poetry, and seem to function as the 'nuts and bolts' of narrative. They are not restricted to descriptive phrases, but can be adverbial—'in days gone by'—or verbal—'he strode beneath the skies'. It has been argued that orally composed poetry is necessarily formulaic—that performer-poets rely on ready-made (or easily adaptable) formulae when they extemporize a text. This view was greatly strengthened by the observation of present-day poet-performers in South-Slavic folk epic traditions, and provided a model for the oral composition of Homeric epic as well as *Beowulf* and other Anglo-Saxon poems.

But it may be felt that terms such as 'formulaic' or 'extemporized' somehow depreciate the poetic quality of a text such as *Beowulf*, and many readers have felt that the theory of oral formulaic composition cannot account for the complexity, subtlety, and considered, stately pace of the poem. And it is true that just as Anglo-Saxon poets may have chosen consciously archaic poetic diction because of conservative poetic habits, so a literate poet may well have chosen to write in an oral formulaic style characteristic of much older poetry. It has certainly been demonstrated that Anglo-Saxon poems which are based on existing Latin written texts show the same oral formulaic stamp as works which, because of their ancient subject matter, might be suspected of having originated in pre-literate times. So perhaps the most we can say is that although *Beowulf* shows some of the stylistic qualities of oral poetry, this may tell us more about the poet's awareness of Old English literary traditions, of his sense of what was an appropriate mode for a long poem dealing with the legendary heroes of the Germanic past, than about the actual origins of the text.

It is very probable, however, that *Beowulf* was intended for recitation rather than for silent reading. Alcuin's letter plainly refers to a listening audience for heroic poetry, and the poem's opening command—'Hwæt' (Listen!)—confirms this, even if there are no clues in the poem itself about whether such an audience would have been clerical or courtly. In fact, the whole text of *Beowulf* comprises an intricate pattern of oral recitations; one might say that one of the poem's themes is the performance of poetry, and that it is therefore a classically self-referential work, that is, one which mirrors its own formal essence in its subject matter.

## Narrative Method and the Heroic Tradition

After the opening call for attention, the poet reminds the audience that the material he is about to present—'the daring feats' of the Danish kings—is already familiar to us, presumably from poems just like *Beowulf* itself. Thus *Beowulf* is decisively located in the context of a wider heroic tradition. The chronological account of the Danish royal lineage, the terrorizing of the Danes by Grendel, and the consequent arrival of Beowulf from Geatland, proceed in straightforward sequence. But Beowulf's first challenge in Heorot is not physical, but verbal: Unferth, one of Hrothgar's courtiers, relates a story about Beowulf's youth, accusing him of reckless behaviour. Beowulf defends himself by re-telling the tale with differing emphases; he puts the story right. This odd exchange in fact adumbrates some of the major themes of the poem. Most obviously, it explores the nature of heroism, especially the fine line between discretion and valour, a crucial issue, for Beowulf's last great encounter, with the dragon, leaves him open precisely to the charge of recklessness. But Unferth's challenge also suddenly diverts the progress of the poem from the orderly, sequential recounting of incident to another time and place—Beowulf's youth, and the wild seascape of his swimming contest with a contemporary, Breca —which still has a direct bearing on the central, present moment of the poem's narrative: the arrival of Beowulf in Heorot, and the expectations the Danes have of the hero. The power of the narrative within a narrative to juxtapose time and place in order to bring out some aspect of the story of Beowulf himself gives the poem much of its drama and richness.

When Beowulf has overcome the monster Grendel on his first night in Heorot, the Danes celebrate his achievement in poetic song—just as our poem does—and go on to recite more material about the celebrated legendary hero Sigemund. On one level, a flattering comparison between Beowulf and Sigemund is established (in fact, close attention to the story of Sigemund reveals that Beowulf may come out the more impressive of the two), but on another, an identity is established between heroic poems about Sigemund and the substance of *Beowulf* itself, so that audiences merge: the Danes listen to celebrations of two great heroes, Sigemund and Beowulf, just as we, and the Anglo-Saxon audience, do.

At the feast following Beowulf's victory over Grendel, the Danes again celebrate with heroic song. This time, a story is told

about the battle between Finn, leader of the Frisians and lord of
Finnsburh, and Hnæf, a Dane whose sister Hildeburh is married
to Finn. However, this is not told as an edifying heroic parallel
to the events of the poem, but functions as a piece of ominous
dramatic irony: the poet begins not with the martial valour of the
opposing sides, but with the dreadful grief of Hildeburh, who, in
the light of the morning after the battle, sees that she has been
doubly bereaved: both her brother Hnæf and her young son have
been killed in the fight. When the poet shifts abruptly back to the
celebrations in Heorot, and Hrothgar's queen Wealhtheow is
shown graciously offering wine to her husband and guest, we inevit-
ably make the connection between the two women, both vulner-
able figures in heroic society. But the parallel runs deeper still:
Hrothgar's own daughter, Freawaru, is to be married to Ingeld of
the Heathobards, traditional enemies of the Danes, in a fruitless
conciliatory gesture, and, as Beowulf himself foresees, Freawaru
too will be the victim of the hostility between natal and marital
families, just as Hildeburh has been. The poet of *Beowulf* makes
no comment on these dark connections, but Beowulf's own under-
standing of the relationship between the songs of the past and
contemporary political circumstances, reinforced by Hrothgar's
wise advice, provokes us to think about what lessons *Beowulf* might
have had for an Anglo-Saxon audience—or, indeed, ourselves. As
we see Beowulf correcting Unferth's version of the Breca story, it
is as if we are being shown narrative in the very process of being
refined into its authoritative form. The same process takes place
when Beowulf returns to Geatland; he recounts the story of his
fights with the monsters and adds his own views on the state of
the Danish royal house—including, of course, his pessimistic
predictions about its future. And yet, the very possibility that the
same events may be recounted and interpreted in different ways
raises unsettling questions about the authority and authenticity of
tradition, and the poet's own subject matter.

So far, then, the poem has presented itself as part of a world
of oral storytelling, and, apart from the narratives within the

narrative, it has recounted events in an orderly, chronological way, from the beginning of the Danish royal house to Beowulf's heroic vanquishing of the monsters which threaten it and his triumphant return to Geatland. At this point, however, the narrative takes a great leap forward to a time when Beowulf has been ruling the Geats for fifty years, and is now facing the final challenge of his career. But the early history of the Geats is not merely skipped over; it is told in retrospective snatches, and in reverse chronological order— that is, more recent events are recounted first. It is very hard to conceive of such intricate narrative method taking shape in an oral context. A more pressing question is why the poet abandoned the narrative clarity of the first two-thirds of the poem and took on such a complex method. The answer may be that the poet is show- ing us the relationship between past and present from two per- spectives. He begins by recounting the events which are to shape the notorious future history of the Danish royal house; he con- cludes by revealing how the present vulnerability of the Geatish people has been shaped by events from years past.

The dragon guards a treasure hoard which is the only remaining material evidence of a whole people who have been wiped out by war—just as, so *Beowulf* tells us, the Geats will be after Beowulf's death. The poet imagines a moving speech which the last surviving representative of this people would make as he consigns the trea- sure to the earth: a pseudo-funeral oration, an elegy to a people, indeed a whole world, long past. In a sense, this brief passage is a microcosm of *Beowulf* itself, as well as prefiguring the elegiac eulogies to Beowulf as his ashes and treasure are consigned to the earth at the end of the poem.

As the poet recounts the dramatic encounter between Beowulf and the dragon, he repeatedly breaks off to return to the legacy of past conflicts—the wars between the Geats and the Swedes. At first, he relates how Hygelac, Beowulf's uncle, met his death in a reckless raid on the Franks (a variation of the theme of discretion and valour), how Hygelac's son inherited the Geatish throne, and (perhaps also recklessly) gave refuge to the rebellious nephews of the Swedish king Onela, whose revenge was swift. Then, as Beowulf ponders his imminent encounter with the dragon, he recalls his own childhood, when he was fostered by Hrethel, his grandfather. Hrethel died of a broken heart when one of his sons, Hæthcyn, accidentally killed an elder brother; unable to take revenge Hrethel sank into a disabling paralysis of the will. It was this weakness in the Geatish kingdom which provoked wars between the Swedes and the Geats, and we are thus made aware that Beowulf may be risking the Geatish people in much the same way if he risks his own life by taking on the dragon. But after Beowulf's death, when a Geatish messenger recollects how Ongentheow, the king of the Swedes, killed Hæthcyn, we see the situation in a slightly different light. Ongentheow was retaliating against a reckless first strike against his people. Perhaps we are to understand that without a father's guidance, Hæthcyn failed to temper heroic valour with kingly discretion, and that the whole complex story of this long-running feud again comes down to this crucial calculation. Certainly the Geatish messenger has no doubts about how to read the situation: he predicts that the Swedes will attack the moment they hear of Beowulf's death, and all the evidence provided in *Beowulf* suggests that he is right.

The history of the Swedes and the Geats is a vivid illustration of how history repeats itself, of how the Geatish leaders again and again risk their lives, and the security of the Geatish people, for the bold heroic gesture. This is the context in which we view Beowulf's fight with the dragon, a fight in which Beowulf refuses the help of his retinue and chooses valour over discretion. The heroic ideal seems to demand decisive individual action, but history shows that this is rarely compatible with the mundane business of political leadership.

There are also a number of examples of repeated patterns of personal relationship in *Beowulf*, the most striking being that between uncle and nephew. Beowulf, a loyal nephew to Hygelac, exemplifies the ideal, but in both the Swedish and Danish dynasties this relationship is a site of bitter conflict. For example, the nephews of the Swedish king Onela rebel against their uncle: Onela has one of them killed—even rewarding the killer with the gift of his own nephew's sword—and the other takes revenge by killing Onela in his turn. In Denmark, the hostility is still to come, but easily foreseen: Hrothgar has inherited the Danish throne from his elder brother Heorogar, and we do not know from the poem why Heorogar's son failed to inherit, or what his response to that might have been. Perhaps the poet of *Beowulf* did not know himself— or perhaps the story was too well-known to bear repetition. And present at the Danish court is another of Hrothgar's nephews, Hrothulf, who may also see himself as a contender for the throne. So when Hrothgar's queen Wealhtheow bravely announces at the feast in Heorot that she trusts in their nephew Hrothulf to befriend and support their young sons, the poem's audience does not need to know about the bloody internecine feuding which later Scandinavian sources record to fear the worst about Hrothulf. The relationship between a man and his sister's son was apparently much cherished in Germanic societies; however, it appears from *Beowulf* that for obvious dynastic reasons a brother's son was the last person any ruler could trust.

Patterns such as these may serve as clear directives to the poem's audience, but their function can sometimes be less obvious. We have already seen how Beowulf and the Germanic hero Sigemund are juxtaposed when the poets of Heorot celebrate them both in song; it is a further link between the two dragon-killers that both have younger companions. But while Wiglaf acts staunchly to support Beowulf in his fight with the dragon, Fitela was not there to help Sigemund. Fitela is said to be Sigemund's nephew, but again, Norse sources may illuminate our poem: Fitela was indeed Sigemund's sister's son, but the result of an incestuous relationship between the two. Is this just another variant in the *Beowulf* poet's collection of uncle/nephew relationships? It is interesting that we do not know how Wiglaf is related to Beowulf, beyond the unexpected revelation towards the end of the poem that he and Beowulf belong to the same family, the Wægmundings. But it is the parallel between Beowulf and Sigemund which makes us reconsider Beowulf's relationship with Wiglaf, who, in his heroic support for Beowulf, and stirring rhetoric, shows himself to be Beowulf's spiritual heir.

## History and Myth

It has often been observed that *Beowulf* combines in its narrative two very different kinds of material—essentially, the fabulous and the historical—and that these divisions correspond quite closely to the monster fights on the one hand, and the human feuding on the other. Some readers have felt uncomfortable with the combination, as if the fictionality of the monster fights detracts from the serious business of the history, or the delicate complexity of the history constitutes a tiresome shift from the drama of timeless, mythic encounters between hero and monster. As we have seen, however, *Beowulf* explores the difficulties of operating in both of these spheres; what is fitting behaviour for a young hero—pitting himself against a terrifying scourge—is not necessarily proper for a king on whom a whole people depends for its security. And yet the two worlds of history and myth are not wholly contrastive in the poem. Peace and prosperity are the gifts which both Hrothgar and Beowulf bring to their respective nations, and, in one sense, the monsters in the poem represent the two corresponding threats to heroic society, violence and avarice. We can see Grendel as a sort of hideous nemesis, a physical manifestation of the spirit of violence and feuding which pervades the heroic world, and the fact that this threat is duplicated—in that Grendel's mother returns to Heorot to avenge her son's death—may reflect an obvious truth about the human violence in the poem: that one hostile act engenders another with inexorable causality. The dragon, jealously guarding its gold hoard, and roused to destructive fury by the theft of one item from it, is a symbol of avarice, the vice of a society which lacks social cohesion and confident liberality. These larger correspondences are reinforced by a whole series of detailed analogies which cross the boundaries between the poem's two kinds of subject matter, binding the whole poem into a remarkably dense web of interrelated incident.

Thus, for example, the monstrous behaviour of Grendel and his mother in not only killing but actually eating their victims— Grendel 'bit into [a warrior's] body, drank the blood | from his veins, devoured huge pieces'—is linked on a rhetorical level to the ostensibly mundane fate of Heorot itself: as a result of hostility between the Danes and the Heathobards, Heorot will be destroyed by fire, but the poet describes this as the great hall being *swallowed up* by *tongues* of flame. Similarly, when the bodies of the Finnsburh dead are cremated, the poet describes in shocking detail the *ravenous* flames which *swallow up* the bodies, bone and blood together. Since Grendel and his mother are humanoid monsters, they are inevitably seen as analogous to the humans in the poem, so that their activities, especially Grendel's 'visits' to Heorot, or his mother's murderous grief at his death, invite us to make comparisons between the worlds of the monsters and the heroes. But sometimes these analogies are unexpected, or even disturbing. Grendel is said to be more or less human in form, though gross in size, and he walks upright. Since he uses no weapons in his attacks on the Danes, Beowulf declares that he too will fight without sword and shield, so in this way Beowulf deliberately brings himself down to the monster's level—ironically, in order to enhance his status as hero. However, there are other unsettling connections between Beowulf and Grendel. Beowulf's name— literally, Bee-wolf—may be understood as cryptic circumlocution for 'bear'. Further, we are told in the poem that one of the deeds of Beowulf's youth was the killing of a Frankish warrior, Dæghrefn, who had the life squeezed out of him; he was 'bear-hugged' to death by Beowulf. In this way, Beowulf stands in the liminal space between the two worlds of the poem. Ostensibly, he is part of the historical world, nephew of Hygelac and friend of Hrothgar. But while Hygelac and Hrothgar are known from historical and legendary texts, Beowulf is known only from the poem named after him—

except, crucially, that a figure in a widespread and apparently ancient folk-tale—the so-called 'Bear's Son Tale'—is strikingly reminiscent of Beowulf, not least in his bear-like associations, and he fights a monster in similar circumstances. Once we suggest identification between Beowulf and the shadowy and yet pervasive heroes of folk-tale, it is only a short step further to a fully mythic view of the hero: the age-old conflict between hero and monster which goes back not merely to early Germanic religious practices, as evidenced by the decorations on weaponry dating from earliest times, but beyond that into what has been called the 'universal thought patterns in the human psyche'.[1]

More specific analogues in European literature have often been noted, but have never been clear enough to be cited as either sources or derivatives of the poem itself. The most detailed, and most written-about, parallel is in the fourteenth-century Old Norse text *Grettir's saga*. Its hero Grettir fights two trolls—though here the first is female, and the second male, reversing the order of Beowulf's encounters with Grendel and his mother—and there are a number of very striking similarities of detail, such as the ripping off of the monster's arm, and the hero's descent into an underwater lair. However, the likelihood that the depiction of Beowulf in the poem may be derived from earlier folk-tales is applicable also to Grettir and his saga, so that a definite relationship between saga and poem is hard to formulate. Fresh analogues from amongst a mass of Old Norse legendary sagas are still coming to light, but again folk-tale may be simply a common source, although it does seem that the 'two-troll' version of the monster fight was a Scandinavian speciality. Some scholars have suggested early Irish analogues to the monster fights in *Beowulf*, and there are also parallels in Celtic folk-tales, though these tend to be rather vague.

[1] Margaret Arent, 'The Heroic Pattern: Old Germanic Helmets, *Beowulf* and *Grettis saga*', in Edgar C. Polomé (ed.), *Old Norse Literature and Mythology: A Symposium* (Austin: University of Texas Press, 1969), 130–99.

The question of classical influence raises altogether different difficulties. A number of details in *Beowulf* have been related to the *Odyssey*, and similarities between Homeric and Old English poetic diction have been pointed out. But it is in fact highly unlikely that Homer's work was known in Anglo-Saxon England. Details in *Beowulf* have also been related to Virgil's *Aeneid*, and it has been argued that *Beowulf* owes both the whole concept of historical epic and the presentation of the hero's tragic brilliance to a Virgilian model, although if this were indeed the case one might expect more than the sprinkling of common details which have been proposed.

As has already been indicated, some of the historical material we find in *Beowulf* contains echoes of names and situations in works of Scandinavian legendary history, such as Saxo Grammaticus's *History of the Danes*, written in the early thirteenth century, or in the late Old Norse *Hrólfs saga kraka*. Allusions to the heroic age in Scandinavia are widely scattered in Old Norse poetry and prose, although they do not add up to a coherent picture of the period, changed as they are by literary context and separated by centuries of literary development. The impulse behind the quest to establish analogues is not so much the elucidation of the poem as an attempt to anchor it to a particular cultural or historical context, to establish it as Scandinavian in origin, or tinged with Celtic, or the product of a classically trained literary environment. But as with our inability to fix the poem in any specific Anglo-Saxon time, place, or milieu, so *Beowulf* eludes any attempt to situate its origins in a specific literary tradition.

### The Fight at Finnsburh *and Old English Tradition*

The only substantial analogue to *Beowulf* in Anglo-Saxon literature is a brief fragment of verse extant only in an eighteenth-century transcription and known as *The Fight at Finnsburh*. The fragment plainly treats the fight between Finn and the Danes which is alluded to in *Beowulf*, but in both its narrative detail and its moral perspective on the action it is very different. The episode in *Beowulf* opens as Hildeburh sees that, after fighting between Hnæf and Finn, both her brother and her son by Finn have been killed. As well as Hildeburh's grief, the poem explores the dilemma facing the surviving Danes, led by Hengest: Finn is unable to finish off the fight and rid his hall of the Danes, and they are prevented from returning home by the storms of winter. An uneasy truce is agreed, by which the Danes are promised safe-keeping for the winter, but their situation is humiliatingly close to the circumstances of those held in contempt elsewhere in heroic literature: the retinue which transfers its loyalty from a defeated leader to his victor. Hengest nurses his resentment throughout the winter, but when spring comes, and with it reinforcements, Hengest, taunted by a Danish warrior, leads a sudden counter-attack. The Danes are victorious, Finn is killed, and Hildeburh is taken back to Denmark. The overwhelming impression is of bitterness, grief, and pointless violence. The Danes in the episode are never said to celebrate their eventual triumph (although the Danes at Heorot do), and Hildeburh's response to her return 'home' is not alluded to, unlike the raw references to her grief at the loss of husband, brother, and son.

*The Fight at Finnsburh* begins not in the cold, chill silence of early morning, as Hildeburh surveys the terrible aftermath of the fighting, but, dramatically, with the preceding night attack, in which the moonlight flickering on the weapons of an enemy force might be mistaken for the hall itself burning. All is action and clamour as Hnæf, apparently attacked within a hall by Finn's forces, rouses his men and exhorts them to valour. Bravery in battle, and the loyalty which promotes it, is an end in itself; the poet is all approbation for the way the warriors behave in their five-day fight, and all admiration for the traditional trappings of battle: gleaming swords; the sinister raven, hoping for corpses to feed on; proud expressions of loyalty.

Nothing could illustrate more vividly the special qualities of *Beowulf* than the contrast between the episode and the fragment. In *Beowulf*, the fight at Finnsburh is the occasion for precisely the questioning and exploration of a cultural ideal that has been identified as the hallmark of epic. In the fragment, the darker side of the conflict—the death of warriors—is transformed into an idealized sacrifice in the cause of loyalty and glory. It must of course be recognized that questioning the heroic ideal, and exploring the effect of violent action performed in its name, is necessarily more to the taste of the modern reader than a straightforward celebration of that action would be. The fragment's vivid immediacy and swift, exciting narrative are undeniable literary strengths in themselves, but it is hard to avoid the sense that *The Fight at Finnsburh* is of interest more because it may preserve an example of the 'heroic lay', an early Germanic oral form, than on grounds of its inherent literary merit. What is surprising is that by contrast *Beowulf* itself does not give the impression of being 'walled off from all subsequent times', as one scholar characterizes epic. In fact, presenting the fight at Finnsburh from Hildeburh's point of view is a strategy remarkably appealing to the modern reader.

All this is not to say that *Beowulf* somehow stands apart from the traditions of Old English literature. It is true that no specific, direct links between *Beowulf* and other Old English poems have been established. There is no reference to *Beowulf* in any other known Anglo-Saxon text, and such verbal echoes as there are with other Old English poems are only to be expected, given the formulaic style of the poetry, and cannot indicate with any certainty which work was the borrower and which the lender. But in many respects *Beowulf* is directly comparable with other Old English poems, particularly in mood and treatment. There is a tradition of heroic verse in which the virtues of the warrior, notably the loyalty and courage we see prized in *Beowulf*, are celebrated, and *The Battle of Maldon*, though commemorating a tenth-century encounter between Anglo-Saxons and Norsemen rather than a distant battle from the old heroic age, holds up for admiration the steadfastness of its heroes in the face of defeat. Like *Beowulf*, *The Battle of Maldon* is not wholly uncritical of the actions of the leader, and there is also a strong suggestion of pathos about the death of young warriors, although in the end a loyalty which is in heroically inverse proportion to the likelihood of victory dominates the poem. Two poems, *Widsith* and *Deor*, do relate to an earlier age of Germanic legend, and a number of names in them also occur in *Beowulf*. But neither poem actually elaborates these names beyond the briefest allusion, and in both there is a pervasive sense that they are no more than faint echoes from a distant literary past. There is certainly nothing approaching the fresh, energetic development of material so clear in *Beowulf*.

Elegy might be said to be the dominant mode in Old English secular poetry, and as well as nostalgia for a gloriously anachronistic way of conducting battle in *The Battle of Maldon*, and the faded glamour evoked by the roll-call of heroic legendary names in *Widsith* and *Deor*, the lament for a past which lies at the heart of elegy is most famously expressed in lyric poems such as *The Wanderer*, *The Seafarer*, and *The Wife's Lament*. These poems are celebrated not only for their poignant evocation of a past which contrasts painfully with a harsh present and future, but also for the impression of intimacy in the anonymous speaking voice in each poem; the first-person narrator speaks of his or her own life in deceptively personal terms. Oddly enough, Old English riddles —ostensibly a much more light-hearted genre—also operate with the immediacy of the first-person narrator; the inanimate object which is the solution of the riddle wittily, and sometimes very touchingly, describes its own transformation from raw material into artefact. The high point of this literary technique is the religious poem *The Dream of the Rood*, in which the cross on which Christ was crucified describes not only its transformation from tree to instrument of torture, but also the death of Christ, from its own unique perspective. Just as Christ has been made incarnate, so the Cross, in an equal and opposite transformation, is made animate, and speaks. Twice in *Beowulf* we are reminded of the first-person intimacy of the Anglo-Saxon elegy and riddle: first, at the beginning of the poem, when Beowulf himself solves for Hrothgar's messenger the riddle of who can be leading a large band of armed warriors who have come to Denmark in neither hostility nor exile—

'My name is Beowulf', a version of the concluding line of so many of the Anglo-Saxon riddles—and second, at the end of the poem, when Beowulf describes his childhood, how he was fostered by his grandfather King Hrethel, and began the transformation which has led him to the present moment of the poem's narrative, this final encounter with a dragon in the defence of the Geatish nation.

It has been said of *Beowulf* that the whole poem is an elegy for a lost world by a poet at the height of his culture's literary powers. Certainly, if elegy also demands an individual's personal view of the past, then we can see *Beowulf* as a delicate, interlocking structure of individual perspectives—Hrothgar's recall of the Danes' happier days, Beowulf's report to Hygelac of what happened at Heorot, or his moving retrospection of his own life as he faces the dragon fight—all subsumed under the poet's overarching, all-inclusive depiction of a long-past but treasured age, and transformed into a single perspective by the timeless wisdom of Hrothgar's advice on the transience of earthly glory. In *Beowulf*, the celebratory quality of epic is finely balanced by the valediction of elegy.

# A NOTE ON THE TEXT AND TRANSLATION

Kevin Crossley-Holland's translation conveys very precisely the dual nature of *Beowulf* as both epic and elegy, for the poem's essential dignity is not allowed to come over as stiff splendour or hollow heroics, and does not compromise the human poignancy of the elegiac. Thus, the tone of this translation is remarkably faithful to the original poem. But it may still be useful to include here a short section of the original poem, flanked by a literal, word-for-word translation, and followed by a brief analysis of how the poetry works. It should be remembered that poetic technique, more than any other feature of the poem, places *Beowulf* right at the heart of Anglo-Saxon literary tradition, for the features evident from these opening lines of *Beowulf* are characteristic to some degree of all Old English verse.

| | |
|---|---|
| Hwæt, we Gar-Dena | Listen: we, of the Spear-Danes', |
| in geardagum, | in yore-days, |
| þeodcyninga | of a nation's kings' |
| þrym gefrunon, | glory have heard, |
| hu ða æþelingas | how those princes |
| ellen fremedon. | valour performed. |
| Oft Scyld Scefing | Often Scyld Scefing |
| sceaþena þreatum, | (of) enemies (in) bands |
| monegum mægþum | (from) many races |
| meodosetla ofteah, | mead-benches deprived, |
| egsode eorlas | terrified noble warriors |
| syððan ærest wearð | since first (he) was |
| feasceaft funden; | destitute discovered; |
| he þæs frofre gebad, | he, for that, comfort experienced, |
| weox under weolcnum, | (he) thrived under (the) heavens, |
| weorðmyndum þah, | in   worth-memorials prospered |
| oðþæt him æghwylc þær | until him each-one there |
| ymbsittendra | of neighbouring settlers |

| | | |
|---|---|---|
| ofer hronrade | | over (the) whale-road |
| hyran scolde, | | had to obey, |
| gomban gyldan. | Þæt wæs god | tribute (had) to pay. |
| cyning! | | That was (a) fine king! |

This short opening verse-paragraph, framed by its call for atten-
tion—'Hwæt'—and its concluding judgement—'Þæt wæs god
cyning!'—illustrates the essential features of Old English poetic
style. Each full line falls into two half-lines, commonly separated
in modern editions by a short space which is usually felt to represent
a natural pause in the metre, a caesura. The half-lines are linked
by alliteration: the first accented syllable in each second half-line
begins with the same sound as one or both of the two accented
syllables in the preceding half-line. Thus, in the first full line, 'Gar-
Dena' alliterates with 'geardagum', and in the second, 'þrym' with
'þeodcyninga', while in lines 4–8, each first half-line has two allit-
erating syllables—'Scyld Scefing' or 'feasceaft funden'.

The metrical unit in Old English verse is the half-line; each
half-line has two stressed syllables, with a varying, but limited,
number of unstressed syllables. The alternation of stressed and
unstressed syllables gives each half-line its distinctive rhythm—
sometimes stately and ponderous, sometimes urgent and synco-
pated—and the vast majority of half-lines fall into one of five or
six characteristic metrical patterns. It is the interplay of these met-
rical patterns within the verse paragraph which gives flexibility and
subtlety to the basic two-stress metre. Stress usually falls on the
words with semantic importance—nouns, adjectives, and verbs—
rather than on parts of speech such as articles or prepositions, and
almost always on the semantically important element in the word,
rather than on a grammatical ending or prefix.

The half-line is also the sense unit in Old English verse, and
by comparison with Modern English prose syntax, with its char-
acteristic subject–verb–object sequence, groups of half-lines are
very loosely connected and ordered within the verse paragraph (by
modern standards, there is very little punctuation in the *Beowulf*

manuscript). Often, parallel sentence elements are repeated; this technique is known as variation, and gives the poetry great descriptive richness. Thus, Scyld Scefing, a single subject in a single half-line, is said to act with hostility to his enemies, but we are given two parallel half-lines denoting the hostile actions—he both took away mead-benches and terrified warriors—and two parallel half-lines describing the enemies—they were enemies in bands, and from many races. There is no explicit link to confine one action to one object. Similarly, Scyld's success is detailed in three parallel half-lines: he experienced comfort, thrived under the heavens, and prospered in honour. But simple juxtaposition allows for a considerable degree of flexibility in meaning: are Scyld's three benefits to be understood as a direct result of his aggression, or are they simply a fitting, contrasting recompense for his miserable origins? Or both? Such syntactic fluidity is used to great effect in *Beowulf*.

A number of words in *Beowulf* are found in Old English only in poetry; some, such as 'meodosetl' (mead-bench) in this passage, are found only in *Beowulf* itself. About a third of the lexicon of *Beowulf* consists of compound words, and the economy with which a complex meaning can be conveyed by the direct juxtaposition of the two elements of a compound—as with 'weorðmynd', honour-memorial, or the good opinion or reputation of a person which is held in the minds of others—is comparable to the effect of the juxtaposed half-lines themselves. The most densely packed kind of compound in Old English verses is the kenning, of which the word 'hronrad' (whale-road) is an example here. The meaning is not difficult to grasp (though some kennings, especially in Old Norse literature, are extremely cryptic): what is denoted is the sea. But the kenning is almost a contradiction in its own terms, for the sea is in some respects the opposite of a road, which is land-based. We can only understand sea as road from the perspective of the whale, whose element it is. As land-based humans, then, we recognize that to journey over the sea is to venture into an alien element; the compound 'whale-road' is not merely a verbal flourish, a decorative puzzle, but a significant addition to the meaning of the passage. Thus, in syntax and diction, Old English poetry is both tightly compacted and freely allusive; reading it in the original demands the concentrated focus of puzzle solving as well as the associative skills of the lateral thinker.

*Note: Line numbers in running heads refer to the original poem*

# SELECT BIBLIOGRAPHY

## Editions

Jack, George, *Beowulf: A Student Edition* (Oxford, 1994). This edition (which includes the text of *The Fight at Finnsburh*) has a running glossary alongside the text, and is fully annotated, making it possible for those with only a rudimentary knowledge of Old English to read the poem in the original. The bibliography is extremely useful.

Klaeber, Fr., *Beowulf and the Fight at Finnsburg* (3rd edn., Boston, 1950).

Wrenn, C. L., *Beowulf with the Finnesburg Fragment* (2nd edn., revised by W. F. Bolton, London, 1973; 5th edn., Exeter, 1996).

An accessible facsimile of the original manuscript, with a facing transcription, is J. Zupitsa, *Beowulf* (The Early English Text Society, os 245, London, 1959, with an Introductory Note by N. Davis; repr. 1967) (but see below under Websites).

## Studies on Beowulf

There has been an enormous amount written on *Beowulf*. The best guide to the scholarship on the poem is: R. E. Bjork and J. D. Niles (eds.), *A Beowulf Handbook* (Exeter, 1996), a collection of short essays surveying the history of various aspects of *Beowulf* scholarship (metre, history, gender roles, sources, and so on) followed by chronological bibliographies. This is a very valuable tool for further reading on the poem. Other useful bibliographical aids are: S. B. Greenfield and F. C. Robinson, *A Bibliography of Publications on Old English Literature to the End of 1972* (Toronto, 1980), and the annual bibliographies published in the journal *Anglo-Saxon England*.

Some of the most influential literary critical studies of *Beowulf* are:

Bonjour, A., *The Digressions in Beowulf* (Oxford, 1950).

Brodeur, A. G., *The Art of Beowulf* (Berkeley and Los Angeles, 1959).

Chambers, R. W., *Beowulf: An Introduction*, 3rd edn. with a supplement by C. L. Wrenn (Cambridge, 1959).

Irving, E. B., Jr. *A Reading of Beowulf* (New Haven, 1968).

## Select Bibliography

Robinson, F. C., *Beowulf and the Appositive Style* (Knoxville, 1985).

Sisam, K., *The Structure of Beowulf* (Oxford, 1965).

L. E. Nicholson (ed.), *An Anthology of Beowulf Criticism* (Notre Dame, Ind., 1963, repr. 1976) includes many important articles on the poem, notably J. R. R. Tolkien's 'The Monsters and the Critics', first published in *Proceedings of the British Academy*, XXII (1936), and perhaps the single most celebrated piece of literary criticism of the poem. Two especially valuable articles by historians are: M. Lapidge, '"Beowulf", Aldhelm, the "Liber Monstrorum" and Wessex', *Studi Medievali*, 23 (1982), 151–92, and P. Wormald, 'Bede, "Beowulf" and the Conversion of the Anglo–Saxon Aristocracy', in *Bede and Anglo–Saxon England*, ed. R. T. Farrell (Oxford, 1978), 32–95.

## Background Reading

Bruce-Mitford, R. L. S., *The Sutton Hoo Ship Burial: A Handbook* (London, 1968, 3rd edn. 1979): an account of archaeological finds which have seemed to many to illuminate the material world of *Beowulf*.

Campbell, James, *The Anglo-Saxons* (Oxford, 1982; repr. New York, 1991): a scholarly illustrated history.

Crossley-Holland, Kevin, *The Anglo-Saxon World* (Woodbridge, 1982, repr. Oxford, 1984), contains a wide selection of texts and extracts, literary, historical, and religious, translated from Old English. Amongst the poems translated are: *Deor, The Wanderer, The Seafarer, The Battle of Maldon, Wulf and Eadwacer, Caedmon's Hymn*, and a number of Riddles.

Godden, M., and Lapidge, M. (eds.), *The Cambridge Companion to Old English Literature* (Cambridge, 1991): a collection of introductory essays (including one on *Beowulf* by F. C. Robinson) by leading scholars in the field.

Hamer, Richard, *A Choice of Anglo-Saxon Verse* (London, 1970): most of the most celebrated Anglo-Saxon short poems, with a parallel verse translation on each facing page.

Mitchell, Bruce, *An Invitation to Old English and Anglo-Saxon England* (Oxford, 1995): both a user-friendly guide to learning the Old English language, and a wide-ranging and engaging introduction to Old English literature and Anglo-Saxon culture.

C. M. Bowra, *Heroic Poetry* (London, 1952), W. P. Ker, *Epic and Romance* (London 1908; repr. New York, 1957), A. B. Lord, *The Singer of Tales* (Cambridge, Mass., 1960), and J. M. Foley, *Immanent Art: From Structure to Meaning in Traditional Oral Epic* (Bloomington, Ind., 1991) all put *Beowulf* in the context of oral epic poetry.

## Related Texts and Analogues

*The Anglo-Saxon Chronicle*, trans. and ed. Michael Swanton (London, 1996).

Bede, *The Ecclesiastical History of the English People*, trans. Bertram Colgrave, ed. Judith McClure and Roger Collins (Oxford, 1994).

Boethius, *The Consolation of Philosophy*, trans. V. E. Watts (Harmondsworth, 1969).

Garmonsway, G. N., and Simpson, J., *Beowulf and its Analogues* (London, 1968), an invaluable collection of translations of many texts related to *Beowulf.*

Gregory of Tours, *History of the Franks*, trans. Lewis Thorpe (Harmondsworth, 1974).

*Grettir's saga*, trans. Denton Fox and Hermann Pálsson (Toronto, 1974, repr. 1981).

*Hrafnkel's Saga and other Icelandic Stories*, trans. Hermann Pálsson (Harmondsworth, 1971, repr. 1976).

*The Poetic Edda*, ed. and trans. U. Dronke (Vols. I and II, Oxford, 1969, 1997). Vol. II includes *Völundarkviða*, and a valuable discussion of the Franks Casket.

*The Poetic Edda*, trans. Carolyne Larrington (Oxford, 1996), with Snorri's *Edda* (below), the basic source for Old Norse mythology.

Saxo Grammaticus, *History of the Danes*, the first nine books, trans. Peter Fisher, ed. Hilda Ellis Davidson (Woodbridge, 1979).

Snorri Sturluson's *Edda*, trans. Anthony Faulkes (London, 1987; repr. 1992).

Tacitus, *The Agricola and the Germania*, trans. H. Mattingly, rev. S. A. Handford (Harmondsworth, 1970).

*Völsunga saga*, trans. Jesse Byock (Enfield, 1993).

*Widsith: A Study in Old English Heroic Legend*, R. W. Chambers (Cambridge, 1912).

## Select Bibliography

### Websites

A complete digital facsimile of the *Beowulf* manuscript is a forth-coming electronic publication of the British Library. For an overview of the project, and a good number of pre-publication samplers, see

[http://www.bl.uk/diglib/beowulf/]

The University of Georgetown's Labyrinth Library contains a selection of Old English texts online, including a scholarly edition of *Beowulf*; see

[http://www.georgetown.edu/labyrinth/labyrinth-home.html]

and the complete corpus of Old English as well as editions of *Beowulf* are available online from The Oxford Text Archive

[http://sable.ox.ac.uk/ota/]

The Old English section of ORB (the On-Line Reference Book for Medieval Studies, edited by Cathy Ball) is rightly described online as 'an encyclopaedic compendium of resources for the study of Old English and Anglo-Saxon England'; see

[http://orb.rhodes.edu/encyclop/culture/lit/oldeng.html]

# TIME CHART

Though *Beowulf* is timeless, drawing material from the wealth of Anglo-Saxon culture and from many countries, the time chart sets the poem in a historical perspective. The death of Hygelac, King of the Geats, c. AD 521, is the only independently attested historical event in the poem, and so although there are allusions to characters who flourished one or two centuries before that, we can place the main action of the poem in the sixth century. It is uncertain when the poem was composed, but dates from the seventh to the very beginning of the eleventh century have been proposed.

AD

| | |
|---|---|
| 98 | Tacitus writes *Germania* |
| 410 | The fall of Roman Britain |
| 449 | Hengest and Horsa come to England at the invitation of Vortigern, king of the Britons |
| 455 | Hengest and Horsa kill Vortigern |
| c.521 | Hygelac killed in battle against the Frisians |
| 524 | Boethius writes *The Consolation of Philosophy* |
| 563 | St Columba's foundation of Iona |
| 597 | Augustine sent by Pope Gregory to Britain |
| c.625 | Probable date of the Sutton Hoo ship burial |
| 627 | The conversion of King Edwin of Northumbria by Bishop Paulinus |
| 664 | The Synod of Whitby |
| 673–735 | Life of Bede |
| 680 | Cædmon's vision |
| 757–79 | Reign of Offa, King of Mercia |
| 766–814 | Reign of Charlemagne, King of the Franks |
| 787 | First Viking raids on England |
| 793 | Vikings attack Lindisfarne |
| 865 | Arrival in England of the Danish 'Great Army' |

# Time Chart

# GENEALOGICAL TABLES

### The Danish Royal House

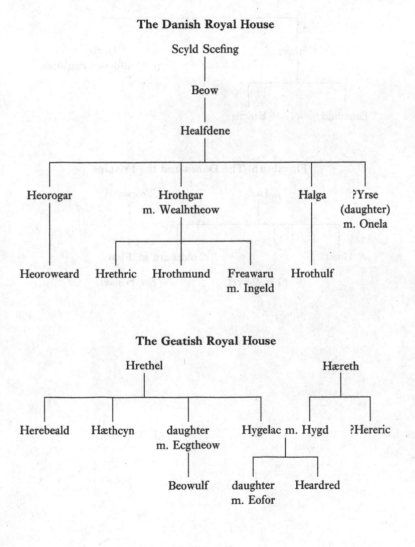

Scyld Scefing

Beow

Healfdene

Heorogar    Hrothgar    Halga    ?Yrse
            m. Wealhtheow        (daughter)
                                 m. Onela

Heoroweard    Hrethric    Hrothmund    Freawaru    Hrothulf
                                       m. Ingeld

### The Geatish Royal House

Hrethel    Hæreth

Herebeald    Hæthcyn    daughter    Hygelac m. Hygd    ?Hereric
                        m. Ecgtheow

Beowulf    daughter    Heardred
           m. Eofor

# Genealogical Tables

## The Swedish Royal House

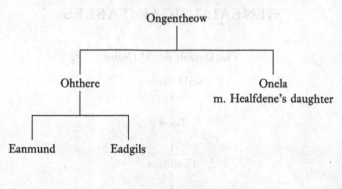

Ongentheow

Ohthere     Onela
m. Healfdene's daughter

Eanmund     Eadgils

## Finnsburh: The Danes and the Frisians

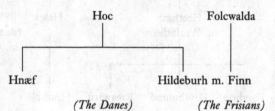

Hoc     Folcwalda

Hnæf     Hildeburh m. Finn

*(The Danes)*     *(The Frisians)*

# BEOWULF

# BEOWULF

Listen!
      The fame of Danish kings
in days gone by, the daring feats
worked by those heroes are well known to us.
  Scyld Scefing* often deprived his enemies,
many tribes of men, of their mead-benches.
He terrified his foes; yet he, as a boy,
had been found a waif; fate made amends for that.
He prospered under heaven, won praise and honour,
until the men of every neighbouring tribe,
across the whale's way, were obliged to obey him
and pay him tribute. He was a noble king!
Then a son was born to him, a child
in the court, sent by God to comfort
the Danes; for He had seen their dire distress,
that once they suffered hardship for a long while,
lacking a lord; and the Lord of Life,
King of Heaven, granted this boy glory;
Beow* was renowned—the name of Scyld's son
became known throughout the Norse lands.
By his own mettle, likewise by generous gifts
while he still enjoys his father's protection,
a young man must ensure that in later years
his companions will support him, serve
their prince in battle; a man who wins renown
will always prosper among any people.

Then Scyld departed at the destined hour,
that powerful man sought the Lord's protection.
His own close companions carried him
down to the sea, as he, lord of the Danes,
had asked while he could still speak.
That well-loved man had ruled his land for many years.
There in harbour stood the ring-prowed ship,
the prince's vessel, icy, eager to sail;
and then they laid their dear lord,
the giver of rings, deep within the ship
by the mast in majesty; many treasures
and adornments from far and wide were gathered there.*
I have never heard of a ship equipped
more handsomely with weapons and war-gear,
swords and corslets; on his breast
lay countless treasures that were to travel far
with him into the waves' domain.
They gave him great ornaments, gifts
no less magnificent* than those men had given him
who long before had sent him alone,
child as he was, across the stretch of the seas.
Then high above his head they placed
a golden banner and let the waves bear him,
bequeathed him to the sea; their hearts were grieving,
their minds mourning. Mighty men
beneath the heavens, rulers in the hall,
cannot say who received that cargo.*

When his royal father had travelled from the earth,
Beow of Denmark, a beloved king,
ruled long in the stronghold, famed
amongst men; in time Healfdene the brave

was born to him; who, so long as he lived,
grey-haired and redoubtable, ruled the noble Danes.
Beow's son Healfdene, leader of men,
was favoured by fortune with four children:
Heorogar and Hrothgar and Halga the good;
Yrse, the fourth, was Onela's queen,
the dear wife of that warlike Swedish king.*

　　Hrothgar won honour in war,
glory in battle, and so ensured
his followers' support—young men
whose number multiplied into a mighty troop.
And he resolved to build a hall,
a large and noble feasting-hall
of whose splendours men would always speak,
and there to distribute as gifts to old and young
all the things that God had given him—
but not men's lives or the public land.
Then I heard that tribes without number, even
to the ends of the earth, were given orders
to decorate the hall. And in due course
(before very long) this greatest of halls
was completed. Hrothgar, whose very word was counted
far and wide as a command, called it Heorot.
He kept his promise, gave presents of rings
and treasure at the feasting. The hall towered high,
lofty and wide-gabled—fierce tongues of loathsome fire
had not yet attacked it, nor was the time yet near
when a mortal feud should flare between father-
and son-in-law, sparked off by deeds of deadly enmity.*

　　Then the brutish demon who lived in darkness
impatiently endured a time of frustration:

[ 4 ]

day after day he heard the din of merry-making
inside the hall, and the sound of the harp
and the bard's clear song. He who could tell
of the origin of men from far-off times lifted his voice,
sang that the Almighty made the earth,
this radiant plain encompassed by oceans:
and that God, all powerful, ordained
sun and moon to shine for mankind,
adorned all regions of the world
with trees and leaves; and sang that He gave life
to every kind of creature that walks about earth.
So those warrior Danes lived joyful lives,
in complete harmony, until the hellish fiend
began to perpetrate base crimes.*
This gruesome creature was called Grendel,
notorious prowler of the borderland, ranger of the moors,
the fen and the fastness; this cursed creature
lived in a monster's lair for a time
after the Creator had condemned him
as one of the seed of Cain—the Everlasting Lord
avenged Abel's murder. Cain had
no satisfaction from that feud, but the Creator
sent him into exile, far from mankind,
because of his crime. He could no longer
approach the throne of grace, that precious place
in God's presence, nor did he feel God's love.*
In him all evil-doers find their origin,
monsters and elves and spiteful spirits of the dead,
also the giants who grappled with God
for a long while; the Lord gave them their deserts.*

    Then, under cover of night, Grendel came

to Hrothgar's lofty hall to see how the Ring-Danes
were disposed after drinking ale all evening;
and he found there a band of brave warriors,
well-feasted, fast asleep, dead to worldly sorrow,
man's sad destiny. At once that hellish monster,
grim and greedy, brutally cruel,
started forward and seized thirty thanes
even as they slept; and then, gloating
over his plunder, he hurried from the hall,
made for his lair with all those slain warriors.
Then at dawn, as day first broke,
Grendel's power was at once revealed;
a great lament was lifted, after the feast
an anguished cry at that daylight discovery.
The famous prince, best of all men, sat apart in mourning;
when he saw Grendel's gruesome footprints,
that great man grieved for his retainers.
This enmity was utterly one-sided, too repulsive,
too long-lasting. Nor were the Danes allowed respite,
but the very next day Grendel committed
violent assault, murders more atrocious than before,
and he had no qualms about it. He was caught up in his crimes.
Then it was not difficult to find the man
who preferred a more distant resting-place,
a bed in the outbuildings, for the hatred
of the hall-warden* was quite unmistakable.
He who had escaped the clutches of the fiend
kept further off, at a safe distance.
 Thus Grendel ruled, resisted justice,
one against all, until the best of halls
stood deserted. And so it remained:

for twelve long winters the lord of the Danes
was sorely afflicted with sorrows and cares;
then men were reminded in mournful songs
that the monster Grendel fought with Hrothgar
for a long time, fought with fierce hatred
committing crime and atrocity day after day
in continual strife. He had no wish for peace
with any of the Danes, would not desist
from his deadly malice or pay *wergild*—*
No! None of the counsellors could hold out hope
of handsome compensation at that slayer's hands.
But the cruel monster constantly terrified
young and old, the dark death-shadow
lurked in ambush; he prowled the misty moors
at the dead of night; men do not know
where such hell-whisperers shrithe* in their wanderings.
Such were the many and outrageous injuries
that the fearful solitary, foe of all men,
endlessly inflicted; he occupied Heorot,
that hall adorned with treasures, on cloudless nights.
This caused the lord of the Danes deep,
heart-breaking grief. Strong men often sat
in consultation, trying in vain to devise
a good plan as to how best valiant men
could safeguard themselves against sudden attack.
At times they offered sacrifices to the idols
in their pagan tabernacles, and prayed aloud
to the soul-slayer that he would assist them
in their dire distress. Such was the custom
and comfort of the heathen; they brooded in their hearts
on hellish things—for the Creator, Almighty God,

the judge of all actions, was neglected by them;
truly they did not know how to praise the Protector of Heaven,
the glorious Ruler.* Woe to the man who,
in his wickedness, commits his soul to the fire's embrace;
he must expect neither comfort nor change.
He will be damned for ever. Joy shall be his
who, when he dies, may stand before the Lord,
seek peace in the embrace of our Father.

Thus Healfdene's son endlessly brooded
over the afflictions of this time; that wise warrior
was altogether helpless, for the hardship upon them—
violent visitations, evil events in the night—
was too overwhelming, loathsome, and long-lasting.

One of Hygelac's thanes, Beowulf by name,
renowned among the Geats for his great bravery,
heard in his own country of Grendel's crimes;
he was the strongest man alive,
princely and powerful. He gave orders
that a good ship should be prepared, said he would sail
over the sea to assist the famous leader,
the warrior king, since he needed hardy men.
Wise men admired his spirit of adventure.
Dear to them though he was, they encouraged
the warrior and consulted the omens.
Beowulf searched out the bravest of the Geats,
asked them to go with him; that seasoned sailor
led fourteen thanes to the ship at the shore.

Days went by; the boat was on the water,
moored under the cliff. The warriors, all prepared,
stepped onto the prow—the water streams eddied,
stirred up sand; the men stowed

gleaming armour, noble war-gear
deep within the ship; then those warriors launched
the well-built boat and so began their journey.
Foaming at the prow and most like a sea-bird,
the boat sped over the waves, urged on by the wind;
until next day, at about the expected time,
so far had the curved prow come
that the travellers sighted land,
shining cliffs, steep hills,
broad headlands. So did they cross the sea;
their journey was at its end. Then the Geats
disembarked, lost no time in tying up
the boat—their corslets clanked;
the warriors gave thanks to God
for their safe passage over the sea.

Then, on the cliff-top, the Danish watchman
(whose duty it was to stand guard by the shore)
saw that the Geats carried flashing shields
and gleaming war-gear down the gangway,
and his mind was riddled with curiosity.
Then Hrothgar's thane leaped onto his horse
and, brandishing a spear, galloped
down to the shore; there, he asked at once:
'Warriors! Who are you, in your coats of mail,
who have steered your tall ship over the sea-lanes
to these shores? I've been a coastguard here
for many years, kept watch by the sea,
so that no enemy band should encroach
upon this Danish land and do us injury.
Never have warriors, carrying their shields,
come to this country in a more open manner.

Nor were you assured of my leaders' approval,
my kinsmen's consent. I've never set eyes
on a more noble man, a warrior in armour,
than one among your band; he's no mere retainer,
so ennobled by his weapons. May his looks never belie him,
and his lordly bearing. But now, before you step
one foot further on Danish land
like faithless spies, I must know
your lineage. Bold seafarers,
strangers from afar, mark my words
carefully: you would be best advised
quickly to tell me the cause of your coming.'*

The man of highest standing, leader of that troop,
unlocked his hoard of words, answered him:
'We are all Geats, hearth-companions of Hygelac;
my father was famed far and wide,
a noble lord, Ecgtheow by name—
he endured many winters before he,
in great old age, went on his way; every wise man
in this world readily recalls him.
We have sailed across the sea to seek your lord,
Healfdene's son, protector of the people,
with most honourable intentions; give us your guidance!
We have come on an errand of importance
to the great Danish prince; nor, I imagine, will the cause
of our coming long remain secret. You will know
whether it is true—as we have heard tell—
that here among the Danes a certain evil-doer,
a fearful solitary, on dark nights commits deeds
of unspeakable malice—damage
and slaughter. In good conscience

I can counsel Hrothgar, that wise and good man,
how he shall overcome the fiend,
and how his anguish shall be assuaged—
if indeed his fate ordains that these foul deeds
should ever end, and be avenged;
he will suffer endless hardship otherwise,
dire distress, as long as Heorot, best of dwellings,
stands unshaken in its lofty place.'
   Still mounted, the coastguard,
a courageous thane, gave him this reply:
'The discriminating warrior—one whose mind is keen—
must perceive the difference between words and deeds.
But I see you are a company well disposed
towards the Danish prince. Proceed, and bring
your weapons and armour! I shall direct you.
And I will command my companions, moreover,
to guard your ship with honour
against any foe—your beached vessel,
so recently caulked—until the day that timbered craft
with its curved prow shall carry back
the beloved man across the sea currents
to the shores of the storm-loving Geats:
he who dares deeds with such audacity and valour
shall be granted safety in the squall of battle.'
   Then they hurried on. The ship lay still;
securely anchored, the spacious vessel
rode on its hawser. The boar crest, brightly gleaming,
stood over their helmets: superbly tempered,
plated with glowing gold, it guarded the lives
of those grim warriors.* The thanes made haste,
marched along together until they could discern

the glorious, timbered hall, adorned with gold;
they saw there the best-known building
under heaven. The ruler lived in it;
its brilliance carried across countless lands.
Then the fearless watchman pointed out the path
leading to Heorot, bright home of brave men,
so that they should not miss the way;
that bold warrior turned his horse, then said:
'I must leave you here. May the Almighty Father,
of His grace, guard you in your enterprise.
I will go back to the sea again,
and there stand watch against marauding bands.'

The road was paved; it showed those warriors
the way. Their corslets were gleaming,
the strong links of shining chain-mail
clinked together. When the sea-stained travellers
had reached the hall itself in their fearsome armour,
they placed their broad shields
(worked so skilfully) against Heorot's wall.
Then they sat on a bench; the brave men's
armour sang. The seafarers' gear
stood all together, a grey-tipped forest
of ash spears; that armed troop was well equipped
with weapons.

Then Wulfgar, a proud warrior,
asked the Geats about their ancestry:
'Where have you come from with these gold-plated shields,
these grey coats of mail, these visored helmets,
and this pile of spears? I am Hrothgar's
messenger, his herald. I have never seen
so large a band of strangers of such bold bearing.

You must have come to Hrothgar's court
not as exiles, but from audacity and high ambition.'*
Then he who feared no man, the proud leader
of the Geats, stern-faced beneath his helmet,
gave him this reply: 'We are Hygelac's
companions at the bench: my name is Beowulf.
I wish to explain to Healfdene's son,
the famous prince, your lord,
why we have come if he, in his goodness,
will give us leave to speak with him.'
Wulfgar replied—a prince of the Vandals,*
his mettle, his wisdom and prowess in battle
were widely recognized: 'I will ask
the lord of the Danes, ruler of the Scyldings,
renowned prince and ring-giver,
just as you request, regarding your journey,
and bring back to you at once whatever answer
that gracious man thinks fit to give me.'
   Then Wulfgar hurried to the place where Hrothgar sat,
grizzled and old, surrounded by his thanes;
the brave man moved forward until he stood
immediately before the Danish lord;
he well knew the customs of warriors.
Wulfgar addressed his friend and leader:
'Geatish men have travelled to this land,
come from far, across the stretch of the seas.
These warriors call their leader Beowulf;
they ask, my lord, that they should be allowed
to speak with you. Gracious Hrothgar,
do not give them *no* for answer.
They, in their armour, seem altogether worthy

of the highest esteem. I have no doubt of their leader's
might, he who has brought these brave men to Heorot.'
Hrothgar, defender of the Danes, answered:
'I knew him when he was a boy;
his illustrious father was called Ecgtheow;
Hrethel the Geat gave him his only daughter
in marriage; now his son, with daring spirit,
has voyaged here to visit a loyal friend.
And moreover, I have heard seafarers say—
men who have carried rich gifts to the Geats
as a mark of my esteem—that in the grasp
of his hand that man renowned in battle
has the might of thirty men. I am convinced
that Holy God, of His great mercy,
has directed him to us West-Danes
and that he means to come to grips with Grendel.
I will reward this brave man with treasures.
Hurry! Tell them to come in and meet
our band of kinsmen; and make it clear, too,
that they are most welcome to the Danes!'
Then Wulfgar went to the hall door with Hrothgar's reply:
'My conquering lord, the leader of the East-Danes
commands me to tell you that he knows your lineage
and that you, so bold in mind, are welcome
to these shores from over the rolling sea.
You may see Hrothgar in your armour,
under your helmets, just as you are;
but leave your shields out here, and your deadly ashen spears,
let them await the outcome of your words.'
    Then noble Beowulf rose from the bench,
flanked by his fearless followers; some stayed behind

at the brave man's bidding, to stand guard over their armour.
Guided by Wulfgar, the rest hurried into Heorot
together; there went that hardy man, stern-faced
beneath his helmet, until he was standing under Heorot's roof.
Beowulf spoke—his corslet, cunningly linked
by the smith, was shining: 'Greetings, Hrothgar!
I am Hygelac's kinsman and retainer. In my youth
I achieved many daring exploits. Word of Grendel's deeds
has come to me in my own country;
seafarers say that this hall Heorot,
best of all buildings, stands empty and useless
as soon as the evening light is hidden under the sky.
So, Lord Hrothgar, men known by my people
to be noble and wise advised me to visit you
because they knew of my great strength:
they saw me themselves when, stained by my enemies' blood,
I returned from the fight when I destroyed five,
a family of giants, and by night slew monsters
on the waves; I suffered great hardship,
avenged the affliction of the Storm-Geats and crushed
their fierce foes—they were asking for trouble.
And now, I shall crush the giant Grendel
in single combat. Lord of the mighty Danes,
guardian of the Scyldings, I ask one favour:
protector of warriors, lord beloved of your people,
now that I have sailed here from so far,
do not refuse my request—that I alone, with my band
of brave retainers, may cleanse Heorot.
I have also heard men say this monster
is so reckless he spurns the use of weapons.
Therefore (so that Hygelac, my lord,

may rest content over my conduct) I deny myself
the use of a sword and a broad yellow shield
in battle; but I shall grapple with this fiend
hand to hand; we shall fight for our lives,
foe against foe; and he whom death takes off
must resign himself to the judgement of God.
I know that Grendel, should he overcome me,
will without dread devour many Geats,
matchless warriors, in the battle-hall,
as he has often devoured Danes before. If death claims me
you will not have to cover my head,
for he already will have done so—
with a sheet of shining blood; he will carry off
the blood-stained corpse, meaning to savour it;
the solitary one will eat without sorrow
and stain his lair; no longer then
will you have to worry about burying my body.
But if battle should claim me, send this most excellent
coat of mail to Hygelac, this best of corslets
that protects my breast; it once belonged to Hrethel,
the work of Weland.* Fate goes ever as it must!'

  Hrothgar, protector of the Scyldings, replied:
'Beowulf, my friend! So you have come here,
because of past favours, to fight on our behalf!
Your father Ecgtheow, by striking a blow,
began the greatest of feuds. He slew Heatholaf of the Wylfings*
with his own hand; after that, the Geats
dared not harbour him for fear of war.
So he sailed here, over the rolling waves,
to this land of the South-Danes, the honoured Scyldings;
I was young then, had just begun to reign

over the Danes in this glorious kingdom,
this treasure-stronghold of heroes; my elder brother,
Heorogar, Healfdene's son, had died
not long before; he was a better man than I!
I settled your father's feud by payment;
I sent ancient treasures to the Wylfings
over the water's back; and Ecgtheow swore oaths to me.*
It fills me with anguish to admit to all the evil
that Grendel, goaded on by his hatred,
has wreaked in Heorot with his sudden attacks
and infliction of injuries; my hall-troop is depleted,
my band of warriors; fate has swept them
into Grendel's ghastly clutches. Yet God can easily
prevent this reckless ravager from committing such crimes.
After quaffing beer, brave warriors of mine
have often boasted over the ale-cup
that they would wait in Heorot
and fight against Grendel with their fearsome swords.
Then, the next morning, when day dawned,
men could see that this great mead-hall was stained
by blood, that the floor by the benches
was spattered with gore; I had fewer followers,
dear warriors, for death had taken them off.
But first, sit down at our feast, and in due course,
as your inclination takes you, tell how warriors
have achieved greatness.'
                  Then, in the feasting-hall,
a bench was cleared for the Geats all together,
and there those brave men went and sat,
delighting in their strength; a thane did his duty—
held between his hands the adorned ale-cup,

poured out gleaming liquor; now and then the poet
raised his voice, resonant in Heorot; the warriors caroused,
no small company of Scyldings and Geats.
Ecglaf's son, Unferth,* who sat at the feet
of the lord of the Scyldings, unlocked his thoughts
with these unfriendly words—for the journey of Beowulf,
the brave seafarer, much displeased him
in that he was unwilling for any man
in this wide world to gain more glory than himself:
'Are you the Beowulf who competed with Breca,*
vied with him at swimming in the open sea
when, swollen with vanity, you both braved
the waves, risked your lives on deep waters
because of a foolish boast? No one,
neither friend nor foe, could keep you
from your sad journey, when you swam out to sea,
clasped in your arms the water-streams,
passed over the sea-paths, swiftly moved your hands
and sped over the ocean. The sea heaved,
the winter flood; for seven nights
you both toiled in the water; but Breca outstayed you,
he was the stronger; and then, on the eighth morning,
the sea washed him up on the shores of the Heathoreams.*
From there he sought his own country,
the land of the Brondings who loved him well;
he went to his fair stronghold where he had a hall
and followers and treasures. In truth, Beanstan's son
fulfilled his boast that he could swim better than you.
So I am sure you will pay a heavy price—
although you have survived countless battle storms,
savage sword-play—if you dare

ambush Grendel in the watches of the night.'*
Beowulf, the son of Ecgtheow, replied:
'Truly, Unferth my friend, all this beer
has made you talkative: you have told us much
about Breca and his exploits. But I maintain
I showed the greater stamina, endured
hardship without equal in the heaving water.
Some years ago when we were young men,
still in our youth, Breca and I made a boast,
a solemn vow, to venture our lives
on the open sea; and we kept our word.
When we swam through the water, we each held
a naked sword with which to ward off
whales; by no means could Breca
swim faster than I, pull away from me
through the press of the waves—
I had no wish to be separated from him.
So for five nights we stayed together in the sea,
until the tides tore us apart,
the foaming water, the freezing cold,
day darkening into night—until the north wind,
that savage warrior, rounded against us.
Rough were the waves; fishes in the sea
were roused to great anger. Then my coat of mail,
hard and hand-linked, guarded me against my enemies;
the woven war-garment, adorned with gold,
covered my breast. A cruel ravager
dragged me down to the sea-bed, a fierce monster
held me tightly in its grasp; but it was given to me
to bury my sword, my battle weapon,
in its breast; the mighty sea-beast

was slain by my blow in the storm of battle.
In this manner, and many times, loathsome monsters
harassed me fiercely; with my fine sword
I served them fittingly.
I did not allow those evil destroyers to enjoy
a feast, to eat me limb by limb
seated at a banquet on the sea-bottom;
but the next morning they lay in the sand
along the shore, wounded by sword strokes,
slain by battle-blades, and from that day on
they could not hinder seafarers from sailing
over deep waters. Light came from the east,
God's bright beacon; the swell subsided,
and I saw then great headlands,
cliffs swept by the wind. Fate will often spare
an undoomed man, if his courage is good.
As it was I slew nine sea-beasts
with my sword. I have never heard
of a fiercer fight by night under heaven's vault
nor of a man who endured more on the ocean streams.
But I escaped with my life from the enemies' clutches,
worn out by my venture.* Then the swift current,
the surging water, carried me
to the land of the Lapps. I have not heard tell
that you have taken part in any such contests,
in the peril of sword-play. Neither you nor Breca
have yet dared such a deed with shining sword
in battle—I do not boast because of this—
though of course it is true you slew your own brothers,
your own close kinsmen.* For that deed, however clever
you may be, you will suffer damnation in hell.

I tell you truly, son of Ecglaf,
that if you were in fact as unflinching
as you claim, the fearsome monster Grendel
would never have committed so many crimes
against your lord, nor created such havoc in Heorot;
but he has found he need not fear unduly
your people's enmity, fearsome assault
with swords by the victorious Scyldings.
So he spares none but takes his toll
of the Danish people, does as he will,
kills and destroys, expects no fight
from the Spear-Danes. But soon, quite soon,
I shall show him the strength, the spirit and skill
of the Geats. And thereafter, when day dawns,
when the radiant sun shines from the south
over the sons of men, he who so wishes
may enter the mead-hall without terror.'

Then the grizzled warrior, giver of gold,
was filled with joy; the lord of the Danes,
shepherd of his people, listened to Beowulf's
brave resolution and relied on his help.
The warriors laughed, there was a hum
of contentment. Wealhtheow came forward,
mindful of ceremonial—she was Hrothgar's queen;
adorned with gold, that proud woman
greeted the men in the hall, then offered the cup
to the Danish king first of all.
She begged him, beloved of his people,
to enjoy the feast; the king, famed
for victory, ate and drank in happiness.
Then the lady of the Helmings walked about the hall,

offering the precious, ornamented cup
to old and young alike, until at last
the queen, excellent in mind, adorned with rings,
moved with the mead-cup towards Beowulf.
She welcomed the Geatish prince and with wise words
thanked God that her wish was granted
that she might depend on some warrior for help
against such attacks. The courageous man
took the cup from Wealhtheow's hands
and, eager for battle, made a speech:
Beowulf, the son of Ecgtheow, said:
'When I put to sea, sailed
through the breakers with my band of men,
I resolved to fulfil the desire
of your people, or suffer the pangs of death,
caught fast in Grendel's clutches.
Here, in Heorot, I shall either work a deed
of great daring, or lay down my life.'
Beowulf's brave boast delighted Wealhtheow:
adorned with gold, the noble Danish queen
went to sit beside her lord.

Then again, as of old, fine words were spoken
in the hall, the company rejoiced,
a conquering people, until in due course
the son of Healfdene wanted to retire
and take his rest. He realized the monster
meant to attack Heorot after the blue hour,
when black night has settled over all—
when shadowy shapes come shrithing
dark beneath the clouds. All the company rose.
Then the heroes Hrothgar and Beowulf saluted

[ 22 ]

one another; Hrothgar wished him luck
and control of Heorot, and confessed:
'Never since I could lift hand and shield,
have I entrusted this glorious Danish hall
to any man as I do now to you.
Take and guard this greatest of halls.
Make known your strength, remember your might,
stand watch against your enemy. You shall have
all you desire if you survive this enterprise.'
    Then Hrothgar, defender of the Danes,
withdrew from the hall with his band of warriors.
The warlike leader wanted to sleep with Wealhtheow,
his queen. It was said the mighty king
had appointed a hall-guard*—a man who undertook
a dangerous duty for the Danish king,
elected to stand watch against the monster.
Truly, the leader of the Geats fervently trusted
in his own great strength and in God's grace.
Then he took off his helmet and his corslet
of iron, and gave them to his servant,
with his superb, adorned sword,
telling him to guard them carefully.
And then, before he went to his bed,
the brave Geat, Beowulf, made his boast:
'I count myself no less active in battle,
no less brave than Grendel himself:
thus, I will not send him to sleep with my sword,
so deprive him of life, though certainly I could.
Despite his fame for deadly deeds,
he is ignorant of these noble arts, that he might strike
at me, and hew my shield; but we, this night,

[ 23 ]

shall forgo the use of weapons, if he dares fight
without them; and then may wise God,
the holy Lord, give glory in battle
to whichever of us He should think fitting.'*
Then the brave prince leaned back, put his head
on the pillow while, around him,
many a proud seafarer lay back on his bed.
Not one of them believed he would see
day dawn, or ever return to his family
and friends, and the place where he was born;
they well knew that in recent days
far too many Danish men had come to bloody ends
in that hall. But the Lord wove the webs of destiny,
gave the Geats success in their struggle,
help and support, in such a way
that all were enabled to overcome their enemy
through the strength of one man. We cannot doubt
that mighty God has always ruled
over mankind.

        Then the night prowler
came shrithing through the shadows. All the Geats
guarding Heorot had fallen asleep—
all except one. Men well knew that the evil enemy
could not drag them down into the shadows
when it was against the Creator's wishes,
but Beowulf, watching grimly for his adversary Grendel,
awaited the ordeal with increasing anger.
Then, under night's shroud, Grendel walked down
from the moors; he shouldered God's anger.
The evil plunderer intended to ensnare
one of the race of men in the high hall.

He strode under the skies, until he stood
before the feasting-hall, in front of the gift-building
gleaming with gold. And this night was not the first
on which he had so honoured Hrothgar's home.
But never in his life did he find hall-wardens
more greatly to his detriment. Then the joyless warrior
journeyed to Heorot. The outer door, bolted
with iron bands, burst open at a touch from his hands:
with evil in his mind, and overriding anger,
Grendel swung open the hall's mouth itself. At once,
seething with fury, the fiend stepped onto
the tessellated floor; a horrible light,
like a lurid flame, flickered in his eyes.
He saw many men, a group of warriors,
a knot of kinsmen, sleeping in the hall.
His spirits leapt, his heart laughed;
the savage monster planned to sever,
before daybreak, the life of every warrior
from his body—he fully expected to eat
his fill at the feast. But after that night
fate decreed that he should no longer feed off
human flesh. Hygelac's kinsman,
the mighty man, watched the wicked ravager
to see how he would make his sudden attacks.
The monster was not disposed to delay;
but, for a start, he hungrily seized
a sleeping warrior, greedily wrenched him,
bit into his body, drank the blood
from his veins, devoured huge pieces;
until, in no time, he had swallowed the whole man,
even his feet and hands. Now Grendel stepped forward,

[ 25 ]

nearer and nearer, made to grasp the valiant Geat
stretched out on his bed—the fiend reached towards him
with his open hand; at once Beowulf perceived
his evil plan, sat up and stayed Grendel's outstretched arm.
Instantly that monster, hardened by crime,
realized that never had he met any man
in the regions of earth, in the whole world,
with so strong a grip.* He was seized with terror.
But, for all that, he was unable to break away.
He was eager to escape to his lair, seek the company
of devils, but he was restrained as never before.
Then Hygelac's brave kinsman bore in mind
his boast: he rose from the bed and gripped
Grendel fiercely. The fiend tried to break free,
his fingers were bursting. Beowulf kept with him.
The evil giant was desperate to escape,
if indeed he could, and head for his lair
in the fens; he could feel his fingers cracking
in his adversary's grip; that was a bitter journey
that Grendel made to the ring-hall Heorot.
The great room boomed; all the proud warriors—
each and every Dane living in the stronghold—
were stricken with panic. The two hall-wardens
were enraged. The building rang with their blows.
It was a wonder the wine-hall withstood
two so fierce in battle, that the fair building
did not fall to earth; but it stood firm,
braced inside and out with hammered
iron bands. I have heard tell that there,
where they fought, many a mead-bench,
studded with gold, started from the floor.

Until that time, elders of the Scyldings
were of the opinion that no man could wreck
the great hall Heorot, adorned with horns,
nor by any means destroy it unless it were gutted
by greedy tongues of flame.* Again and again
clang and clatter shattered the night's silence;
dread numbed the North-Danes, seized all
who heard the shrieking from the wall,
the enemy of God's grisly lay of terror,
his song of defeat, heard hell's captive
keening over his wound. Beowulf held him fast,
he who was the strongest of all men
ever to have seen the light of life on earth.
By no means did the defender of thanes
allow the murderous caller to escape with his life;
he reckoned that the rest of Grendel's days
were useless to anyone. Then, time and again,
Beowulf's band brandished their ancestral swords;
they longed to save the life, if they
so could, of their lord, the mighty leader.
When they did battle on Beowulf's behalf,
struck at the monster from every side,
eager for his end, those courageous warriors
were unaware that no war-sword,
not even the finest iron on earth,
could wound their evil enemy,
for he had woven a secret spell
against every kind of weapon, every battle-blade.*
Grendel's death, his departure from this world,
was destined to be wretched, his migrating spirit
was fated to travel far into the power of fiends.

Then he who for years had committed crimes
against mankind, murderous in mind,
and had warred with God, discovered
that the strength of his body could not save him,
that Hygelac's brave kinsman held his hand
in a vice-like grip; each was a mortal enemy
to the other. The horrible monster
suffered grievous pain; a gaping wound
opened on his shoulder; the sinews sprang apart,
the muscles were bursting. Glory in battle
was given to Beowulf; fatally wounded,
Grendel was obliged to make for the marshes,
head for his joyless lair. He was
well aware that his life's days were done,
come to an end. After that deadly encounter
the desire of every Dane was at last accomplished.*

In this way did the wise and fearless man
who had travelled from far cleanse Hrothgar's hall,
release it from affliction. He rejoiced in his night's work,
his glorious achievement. The leader of the Geats
made good his boast to the East-Danes;
he had removed the cause of their distress,
put an end to the sorrow every Dane had shared,
the bitter grief that they had been constrained
to suffer. When Beowulf, brave in battle,
placed hand, arm and shoulder—Grendel's
entire grasp—under Heorot's spacious roof,
that was evidence enough of victory.

Then I have heard that next morning
many warriors gathered round the gift-hall;
leaders of men came from every region,

from remote parts, to look on the wonder,
the tracks of the monster. Grendel's death
seemed no grievous loss to any of the men
who set eyes on the spoor of the defeated one,
saw how he, weary in spirit, overcome in combat,
fated and put to flight, had made for the lake
of water-demons—leaving tracks of life-blood.

There the water boiled because of the blood;
the fearful swirling waves reared up,
mingled with hot blood, battle gore;
fated, he hid himself, then joyless
laid aside his life, his heathen spirit,
in the fen lair; hell received him there.

After this, the old retainers left the lake
and so did the company of young men too;
brave warriors rode back on their gleaming horses
from this joyful journey. Then Beowulf's exploit
was acclaimed; many a man asserted
time and again that there was no better
shield-bearer in the whole world, to north or south
between the two seas, under the sky's expanse,
no man more worthy of his own kingdom.
Yet they found no fault at all with their friendly lord,
gracious Hrothgar—he was a great king.

At times the brave warriors spurred their bays,
horses renowned for their speed and stamina,
and raced each other where the track was suitable.
And now and then one of Hrothgar's thanes
who brimmed with poetry, and remembered lays,
a man acquainted with ancient traditions
of every kind, composed a new song

in correct metre. Most skilfully that man
began to sing of Beowulf's feat,
to weave words together, and fluently
to tell a fitting tale.

     He recounted all he knew
of Sigemund, the son of Wæls;* many a strange story
about his exploits, his endurance, and his journeys
to earth's ends; many an episode
unknown or half-known to the sons of men, songs
of feud and treachery. Only Fitela knew of these things,
had heard them from Sigemund who liked to talk
of this and that, for he and his nephew
had been companions in countless battles—
they slew many monsters with their swords.
After his death, no little fame attached to Sigemund's name,
when the courageous man had killed the dragon,
guardian of the hoard. Under the grey rock
the son of the prince braved that dangerous deed
alone; Fitela was not with him;
for all that, as fate had it, he impaled
the wondrous serpent, pinned it to the rock face
with his patterned sword; the dragon was slain.*
Through his own bravery, that warrior ensured
that he could enjoy the treasure hoard
at will; the son of Wæls loaded it all
onto a boat, stowed the shining treasure
into the ship; the serpent burned in its own flames.
Because of all his exploits, Sigemund,
guardian of strong men, was the best known
warrior in the world—so greatly had he prospered—
after Heremod's prowess, strength and daring

had been brought to an end, when, battling with giants,
he fell into the power of fiends, and was at once
done to death.* He had long endured
surging sorrows, had become a source
of grief to his people, and to all his retainers.
And indeed, in those times now almost forgotten,
many wise men often mourned that great warrior,
for they had looked to him to remedy their miseries;
they thought that the prince's son would prosper
and attain his father's rank, would protect his people,
their heirlooms and their citadel, the heroes' kingdom,
land of the Scyldings. Beowulf, Hygelac's kinsman,
was much loved by all who knew him,
by his friends; but Heremod was stained by sin.

   Now and then the brave men raced their horses,
ate up the sandy tracks—and they were so absorbed
that the hours passed easily. Stout-hearted warriors
without number travelled to the high hall
to inspect that wonder; the king himself, too,
glorious Hrothgar, guardian of ring-hoards,
came from his quarters with a great company, escorted
his queen and her retinue of maidens into the mead-hall.
Hrothgar spoke—he approached Heorot,
stood on the steps, stared at the high roof
adorned with gold, and at Grendel's hand:
'Let us give thanks at once to God Almighty
for this sight. I have undergone many afflictions,
grievous outrages at Grendel's hands; but God,
Guardian of heaven, can work wonder upon wonder.
Until now, I had been resigned,
had no longer believed that my afflictions

would ever end: this finest of buildings
stood stained with battle-blood,
a source of sorrow to my counsellors;
they all despaired of regaining this hall
for many years to come, of guarding it from foes,
from devils and demons. Yet now one warrior
alone, through the Almighty's power, has succeeded
where we failed for all our fine plans.
Indeed, if she is still alive,
that woman (whoever she was) who gave birth
to such a son, to be one of humankind,
may claim that the Creator was gracious to her
in her child-bearing. Now, Beowulf,
best of men, I will love you in my heart
like a son; keep to our new kinship
from this day on. You shall lack
no earthly riches I can offer you.
Most often I have honoured a man for less,
given treasure to a poorer warrior,
more sluggish in the fight. Through your deeds
you have ensured that your glorious name
will endure for ever. May the Almighty grant you
good fortune, as He has always done before!'
  Beowulf, the son of Ecgtheow, answered:
'We performed that dangerous deed
with good will; at peril we pitted ourselves
against the unknown. I wish so much
that you could have seen him for yourself,
that fiend in his trappings, in the throes of death.
I meant to throttle him on that bed of slaughter
as swiftly as possible, with savage grips,

to hear death rattle in his throat
because of my grasp, unless he should escape me.
But I could not detain him, the Lord
did not ordain it—I did not hold my deadly enemy
firm enough for that; the fiend jerked free
with immense power. Yet, so as to save
his life, he left behind his hand,
his arm and shoulder; but the wretched monster
has bought himself scant respite;
the evil marauder, tortured by his sins,
will not live the longer, but agony
embraces him in its deadly bonds,
squeezes life out of his lungs; and now this creature,
stained with crime, must await the day of judgement
and his just deserts from the glorious Creator.'
    After this, the son of Ecglaf boasted less
about his prowess in battle—when all the warriors,
through Beowulf's might, had been enabled
to examine that hand, the fiend's fingers,
nailed up on the gables. Seen from in front,
each nail, each claw of that warlike,
heathen monster looked like steel—
a terrifying spike. Everyone said
that no weapon whatsoever, no proven sword
could possibly harm it, could damage
that battle-hardened, blood-stained hand.
    Then orders were quickly given for the inside of Heorot
to be decorated; many servants, both men and women,
bustled about that wine-hall, adorned that building
of retainers. Tapestries, worked in gold,
glittered on the walls, many a fine sight

for those who have eyes to see such things.
That beautiful building, braced within
by iron bands, was badly damaged;
the door's hinges were wrenched; when the monster,
damned by all his crimes, turned in flight,
despairing of his life, only the hall roof
remained untouched. Death is not easy
to escape, let him who will attempt it.
Man must go to the grave that awaits him—
fate has ordained this for all who have souls,
children of men, earth's inhabitants—
and his body, rigid on its clay bed,
will sleep there after the banquet.*

          Then it was time
for Healfdene's son to proceed to the hall,
the king himself was eager to attend the feast.
I have never heard of a greater band of kinsmen
gathered with such dignity around their ring-giver.
Then the glorious warriors sat on the benches,
rejoicing in the feast. Courteously
their kinsmen, Hrothgar and Hrothulf,
quaffed many a mead-cup, confident warriors
in the high hall. Heorot was packed
with feasters who were friends; the time was not yet come
when the Scyldings practised wrongful deeds.*
Then Hrothgar gave Beowulf Healfdene's sword,
and a battle banner, woven with gold,
and a helmet and a corslet,* as rewards for victory;
many men watched while the priceless, renowned sword
was presented to the hero. Beowulf emptied
the ale-cup in the hall; he had no cause

to be ashamed at those precious gifts.
There are few men, as far as I have heard,
who have given four such treasures, gleaming with gold,
to another on the mead-bench with equal generosity.
A jutting ridge, wound about with metal wires,
ran over the helmet's crown, protecting the skull,
so that well-ground swords, proven in battle,
could not injure the well-shielded warrior
when he advanced against his foes.
Then the guardian of thanes ordered
that eight horses with gold-plated bridles
be led into the courtyard; onto one was strapped
a saddle, inlaid with jewels, skilfully made.
That was the war-seat of the great king,
Healfdene's son, whenever he wanted
to join in the sword-play. That famous man
never lacked bravery at the front in battle,
when men about him were cut down like corn.
Then the king of the Danes, Ing's descendants,
presented the horses and weapons to Beowulf,
bade him use them well and enjoy them.
Thus the renowned prince, the retainers' gold-warden,
rewarded those fierce sallies in full measure,
with horses and treasure, so that no man
would ever find reason to reproach him fairly.
Furthermore, the guardian of warriors gave
a treasure, an heirloom at the mead-bench,
to each of those men who had crossed the sea
with Beowulf; and he ordered that gold
be paid for that warrior Grendel slew
so wickedly—as he would have slain many another,

had not foreseeing God and the warrior's courage
together forestalled him. The Creator ruled over
all humankind, even as He does today.
Wherefore a wise man will value forethought
and understanding. Whoever lives long
on earth, endures the unrest of these times,
will be involved in much good and much evil.

    Then Hrothgar, leader in battle, was entertained
with music—harp and voice in harmony.
The strings were plucked, many a song rehearsed,
when it was the turn of Hrothgar's poet
to please men at the mead-bench, perform in the hall.
He sang of Finn's troop, victims of surprise attack,
and of how that Danish hero, Hnæf of the Scyldings,
was destined to die among the Frisian slain.*

    Hildeburh, indeed, could hardly recommend
the honour of the Jutes; that innocent woman
lost her loved ones, son and brother,
in the shield-play; they fell, as fate ordained,
stricken by spears; and she was stricken with grief.*
Not without cause did Hoc's daughter
mourn the shaft of fate, for in the light of morning
she saw that her kin lay slain under the sky,
the men who had been her endless pride
and joy. That encounter laid claim
to all but a few of Finn's thanes,
and he was unable to finish that fight
with Hnæf's retainer, with Hengest in the hall,
unable to dislodge the miserable survivors;
indeed, terms for a truce were agreed:
that Finn should give up to them another hall,

with its high seat, in its entirety,
which the Danes should own in common with the Jutes;*
and that at the treasure-giving the son of Folcwalda
should honour the Danes day by day,
should distribute rings and gold-adorned gifts
to Hengest's band and his own people in equal measure.
Both sides pledged themselves to this peaceful
settlement. Finn swore Hengest solemn oaths
that he would respect the sad survivors
as his counsellors ordained, and that no man there
must violate the covenant with word or deed,
or complain about it, although they
would be serving the slayer of their lord
(as fate had forced those lordless men to do);*
and he warned the Frisians that if, in provocation,
they should mention the murderous feud,
the sword's edge should settle things.
The funeral fire was prepared, glorious gold
was brought up from the hoard: the best of Scyldings,
that race of warriors, lay ready on the pyre.
Blood-stained corslets, and images of boars*
(cast in iron and covered in gold)
were plentiful on that pyre, and likewise the bodies
of many retainers, ravaged by wounds;
renowned men fell in that slaughter.
Then Hildeburh asked that her own son
be committed to the flames at her brother's funeral,
that his body be consumed on Hnæf's pyre.*
That grief-stricken woman keened over his corpse,
sang doleful dirges. The warriors' voices
soared towards heaven. And so did the smoke

from the great funeral fire that roared
before the barrow; heads sizzled,
wounds split open, blood burst out
from battle scars. The ravenous flames
swallowed those men whole, made no distinction
between Frisians and Danes; the finest men departed.*
Then those warriors, their friends lost to them,
went to view their homes, revisit the stronghold
and survey the Frisian land. But Hengest
stayed with Finn, in utter dejection, all through
that blood-stained winter. And he dreamed
of his own country, but he was unable to steer
his ship homeward, for the storm-beaten sea
wrestled with the wind; winter sheathed the waves
in ice—until once again spring made its sign
(as still it does) among the houses of men:
clear days, warm weather, in accordance as always
with the law of the seasons. Then winter was over,
the face of the earth was fair; the exile
was anxious to leave that foreign people
and the Frisian land. And yet he brooded
more about vengeance than about a voyage,
and wondered whether he could bring about a clash
so as to repay the sons of the Jutes.*
Thus Hengest did not shrink from the duty of vengeance
after Hunlafing had placed the flashing sword,
finest of all weapons, on his lap;
this sword's edges had scarred many Jutes.
And so it was that cruel death by the sword later
cut down the brave warrior Finn in his own hall,
after Guthlaf and Oslaf, arrived from a sea-journey,

had fiercely complained of that first attack,
condemned the Frisians on many scores:
the Scyldings' restless spirits could no longer
be restrained. Then the hall ran red with the blood
of the enemy—Finn himself was slain,
the king with his troop, and Hildeburh was taken.
The Scylding warriors carried that king's
heirlooms down to their ship,
all the jewels and necklaces they discovered
at Finn's hall. They sailed over the sea-paths,
brought that noble lady back to Denmark
and her own people.*

          Thus was the lay sung,
the song of the poet. The hall echoed with joy,
waves of noise broke out along the benches;
cup-bearers carried wine in glorious vessels.
Then Wealhtheow, wearing her golden collar, walked
to where Hrothgar and Hrothulf were sitting side by side,
uncle and nephew, still friends together, true to one another.
And the spokesman Unferth sat at the feet
of the Danish lord; all men admired
his spirit and audacity, although he had deceived
his own kinsmen in a feud.* Then the lady of the Scyldings
spoke these words: 'Accept this cup, my loved lord,
treasure-giver; O gold-friend of men,
learn the meaning of joy again, and speak words
of gratitude to the Geats, for so one ought to do.
And be generous to them too, mindful of gifts
which you have now amassed from far and wide.
I am told you intend to adopt this warrior,
take him for your son. This resplendent ring-hall,

Heorot, has been cleansed; give many rewards
while you may, but leave this land and the Danish people
to your own descendants when the day comes
for you to die.* I am convinced
that gracious Hrothulf will guard our children
justly, should he outlive you, lord of the Scyldings,
in this world; I believe he will repay our sons
most generously if he remembers all we did
for his benefit and enjoyment when he was a boy.'*
Then Wealhtheow walked to the bench where her sons,
Hrethric and Hrothmund, sat with the sons of thanes,
fledgling warriors; where also that brave man,
Beowulf of the Geats, sat beside the brothers.
To him she carried the cup, and asked in gracious words
if he would care to drink; and to him she presented
twisted gold with courtly ceremonial—
two armlets, a corslet and many rings,
and the most handsome collar in the world.
I have never heard that any hero had a jewel
to equal that, not since Hama made off
for his fortress with the Brosings' necklace; that pendant
in its precious setting; he fled from the enmity
of underhand Ermenaric, he chose long-lasting gain.
Hygelac the Geat, grandson of Swerting,
wore that necklace on his last raid
when he fought beneath his banner to defend his treasure,
his battle spoils; fate claimed him then,
when he, foolhardy, courted disaster,
a feud with the Frisians.* On that occasion the famous prince
had carried the treasure, the priceless stones,
over the cup of the waves; he crumpled under his shield.

Then the king's body fell into the hands of Franks,
his coat of mail and the collar also;
after that battle, weaker warriors picked at
and plundered the slain; many a Geat lay dead, guarding
that place of corpses.
                  Applause echoed in the hall.
Wealhtheow spoke these words before the company:
'May you, Beowulf, beloved youth, enjoy
with all good fortune this necklace and corslet,
treasures of the people; may you always prosper;
win renown through courage, and be kind in your counsel
to these boys; for that, I will reward you further.
You have ensured that men will always sing
your praises, even to the ends of the world,
as far as oceans still surround cliffs,
home of the winds. May you thrive, O prince,
all your life. I hope you will amass
a shining hoard of treasure. O happy Beowulf,
be gracious in your dealing with my sons.
Here, each warrior is true to the others,
gentle of mind, loyal to his lord;
the thanes are as one, the people all alert,
the warriors have drunk well. They will do as I ask.'
    Then Wealhtheow retired to her seat
beside her lord. That was the best of banquets,
men drank their fill of wine; they had not tasted
bitter destiny, the fate that had come and claimed
many of the heroes at the end of dark evenings,
when Hrothgar the warrior had withdrawn
to take his rest.* Countless retainers
defended Heorot as they had often done before;

benches were pushed back; the floor was padded
with beds and pillows. But one of the feasters
lying on his bed was doomed, and soon to die.
They set their bright battle-shields
at their heads. Placed on the bench
above each retainer, his crested helmet,
his linked corslet and sturdy spear-shaft,
were plainly to be seen. It was their habit,
both at home and in the field,
to be prepared for battle always,
for any occasion their lord might need
assistance; that was a loyal band of retainers.

    And so they slept. One man paid a heavy price
for his night's rest, as often happened
after Grendel first held the gold-hall
and worked his evil in it, until he met his doom,
death for his crimes. For afterwards it became clear,
and well known to the Scyldings, that some avenger
had survived the evil-doer, still lived after
that grievous, mortal combat.
                    Grendel's mother
was a monster of a woman; she mourned her fate—
she who had to live in the terrible lake,
the cold water streams, after Cain slew
his own brother, his father's son,
with a sword; he was outlawed after that;
a branded man, he abandoned human joys,
wandered in the wilderness. Many spirits, sent
by fate, issued from his seed; one of them, Grendel,
that hateful outcast, was surprised in the hall
by a vigilant warrior spoiling for a fight.

Grendel gripped and grabbed him there,
but the Geat remembered his vast strength,
that glorious gift given him of God,
and put his trust for support and assistance
in the grace of the Lord; thus he overcame
the envoy of hell, humbled his evil adversary.
So the joyless enemy of mankind journeyed
to the house of the dead. And then Grendel's mother,
mournful and ravenous, resolved to go
on a grievous journey to avenge her son's death.*

   Thus she reached Heorot; Ring-Danes, snoring,
were sprawled about the floor. The thanes suffered
a serious reverse as soon as Grendel's mother
entered the hall. The terror she caused,
compared to her son, equalled the terror
an Amazon inspires as opposed to a man,*
when the ornamented sword, forged on the anvil,
the razor-sharp blade stained with blood,
shears through the boar-crested helmets of the enemy.
Then swords were snatched from benches, blades
drawn from scabbards, many a broad shield
was held firmly in the hall; none could don helmet
or spacious corslet—that horror caught them by surprise.
The monster wanted to make off for the moors,
fly for her life, as soon as she was found out.
Firmly she grasped one of the thanes
and made for the fens as fast as she could.
That man whom she murdered even as he slept
was a brave shield-warrior, a well-known thane,
most beloved by Hrothgar of all his hall retainers
between the two seas. Beowulf was not there;

the noble Geat had been allotted another lodging
after the giving of treasure earlier that evening.
Heorot was in uproar; she seized her son's
blood-crusted hand; anguish once again
had returned to the hall. What kind of bargain
was that, in which both sides forfeited
the lives of friends?
                              Then the old king,
the grizzled warrior, was convulsed with grief
when he heard of the death of his dearest retainer.

Immediately Beowulf, that man blessed with victory,
was called to the chamber of the king. At dawn
the noble warrior and his friends, his followers,
hurried to the room where the wise man was waiting,
waiting and wondering whether the Almighty
would ever allow an end to their adversity.
Then Beowulf, brave in battle, crossed
the floor with his band—the timbers thundered—
and greeted the wise king, overlord of Ing's
descendants; he asked if the night had passed off
peacefully, since his summons was so urgent.

Hrothgar, guardian of the Scyldings, said:
'Do not speak of peace; grief once again
afflicts the Danish people. Yrmenlaf's
elder brother, Æschere, is dead,
my closest counsellor and my comrade,
my shoulder-companion when we shielded
our heads in the fight, when soldiers clashed on foot,
slashed at boar-crests. Æschere was all
that a noble man, a warrior should be.
The wandering, murderous monster slew him

[ 44 ]

in Heorot; and I do not know where that ghoul,
drooling at her feast of flesh and blood,
made off afterwards. She has avenged her son
whom you savaged yesterday with vice-like holds
because he had impoverished and killed my people
for many long years. He fell in mortal combat,
forfeit of his life; and now another mighty
evil ravager has come to avenge her kinsman;
and many a thane, mournful in his mind
for his treasure-giver, may feel she has avenged
that feud already, indeed more than amply;
now that hand lies still which once sustained you.

I have heard my people say,
men of this country, counsellors in the hall,
that they have seen *two* such beings,
equally monstrous, rangers of the fell-country,
rulers of the moors; and these men assert
that so far as they can see one bears
a likeness to a woman; grotesque though he was,
the other who trod the paths of exile looked like a man,
though greater in height and build than a goliath;
he was christened *Grendel* by my people
many years ago; men do not know if he
had a father, a fiend once begotten
by mysterious spirits.* These two live
in a little-known country, wolf-slopes, windswept headlands,
perilous paths across the boggy moors, where a mountain stream
plunges under the mist-covered cliffs,
rushes through a fissure. It is not far from here,
if measured in miles, that the lake stands
shadowed by trees stiff with hoar-frost.

[ 45 ]

A wood, firmly-rooted, frowns over the water.
There, night after night, a fearful wonder may be seen—
fire on the water; no man alive
is so wise as to know the nature of its depths.
Although the moor-stalker, the stag with strong horns,
when harried by hounds will make for the wood,
pursued from afar, he will succumb
to the hounds on the brink, rather than plunge in
and save his head. That is not a pleasant place.
When the wind arouses the wrath of the storm,
whipped waves rear up black from the lake,
reach for the skies, until the air becomes misty,
the heavens weep.* Now, once again, help may be had
from you alone. As yet, you have not seen the haunt,
the perilous place where you may meet this most evil monster
face to face. Do you dare set eyes on it?
If you return unscathed, I will reward you
for your audacity, as I did before,
with ancient treasures and twisted gold.'

   Beowulf, the son of Ecgtheow answered:
'Do not grieve, wise Hrothgar! Better each man
should avenge his friend than deeply mourn.*
The days on earth for every one of us
are numbered; he who may should win renown
before his death; that is a warrior's
best memorial when he has departed from this world.*
Come, O guardian of the kingdom, let us lose
no time but track down Grendel's kinswoman.
I promise you that wherever she turns—
to honeycomb caves, to mountain woods,
to the bottom of the lake—she shall find no refuge.

Shoulder your sorrows with patience
this day; this is what I expect of you.'
    Then the old king leaped up, poured out his gratitude
to God Almighty for the Geat's words.
Hrothgar's horse, his stallion with plaited mane,
was saddled and bridled; the wise ruler
set out in full array; his troop of shield-bearers
fell into step. They followed the tracks
along forest paths and over open hill-country
for mile after mile; the monster had made
for the dark moors directly, carrying the corpse
of the foremost thane of all those
who, with Hrothgar, had guarded the hall.
Then the man of noble lineage left Heorot far behind,
followed narrow tracks, string-thin paths
over steep, rocky slopes—remote parts
with beetling crags and many lakes
where water-demons lived. He went ahead
with a handful of scouts to explore the place;
all at once he came upon a dismal wood,
mountain trees standing on the edge
of a grey precipice; the lake lay beneath,
blood-stained and turbulent. Then Danish retainers
were utterly appalled when they came upon
the severed head of their comrade Æschere
on the steep slope leading down to the lake;
all the thanes were deeply distressed.
    The water boiled with blood, with hot gore;
the warriors gaped at it. At times the horn sang
an eager battle-song. The brave men all sat down;
then they saw many serpents in the water,

strange sea-dragons swimming in the lake,
and also water-demons, lying on cliff-ledges,
monsters and serpents of the same kind
as often, in the morning, bring sorrow to ships
on the sail-road.* They plunged to the lake bottom,
bitter and resentful, rather than listen
to the song of the horn. The leader of the Geats
picked off one with his bow and arrow,
ended its life; the metal tip
stuck in its vitals; it swam more sluggishly
after that, as the life-blood ebbed from its body;
in no time this strange sea-dragon
bristled with barbed boar-spears, was subdued
and drawn up onto the cliff; men examined
that disgusting enemy.
                    Beowulf donned
his coat of mail, did not fear for his own life.
His massive corslet, linked by hand
and skilfully adorned, was to essay the lake—
it knew how to guard the body, the bone-chamber,
so that his foe's grasp, in its malicious fury,
could not crush his chest, squeeze out his life;
and his head was guarded by the gleaming helmet
which was to explore the churning waters,
stir their very depths; gold decorated it,
and it was hung with chain-mail as the weapon-smith
had wrought it long before, wondrously shaped it
and beset it with boar-images, so that
afterwards no battle-blade could do it damage.
Not least amongst his mighty aids was Hrunting,
the long-hilted sword Unferth lent him in his need;

it was one of the finest of heirlooms; the iron blade
was engraved with deadly, twig-like patterning,
tempered with battle-blood. It had not failed
any of those men who had held it in their hands,
risked themselves on hazardous exploits,
pitted themselves against foes. That was not
the first time it had to do a hard day's work.
Truly, when Ecglaf's son, himself so strong,
lent that weapon to his better as a swordsman,
he had forgotten all those taunts he flung
when tipsy with wine; he dared not chance
his own arm under the breakers, dared not
risk his life; at the lake he lost
his renown for bravery. It was not so with Beowulf
once he had armed himself for battle.

    The Geat, son of Ecgtheow, spoke:
'Great son of Healfdene, gracious ruler,
gold-friend of men, remember now—
for I am now ready to go—
what we agreed if I, fighting on your behalf,
should fail to return: that you would always
be like a father to me after I had gone.
Guard my followers, my dear friends,
if I die in battle; and, beloved Hrothgar,
send to Hygelac the treasures you gave me.
When the lord of the Geats, Hrethel's son,
sees those gifts of gold, he will know
that I found a noble giver of rings
and enjoyed his favour for as long as I lived.
And, O Hrothgar, let renowned Unferth
have the ancient treasure, the razor sharp

ornamented sword; and I will make my name
with Hrunting, or death will destroy me.'

After these words the leader of the Geats
dived bravely from the bank, did not even
wait for an answer; the seething water
received the warrior. A full day elapsed
before he could discern the bottom of the lake.*

She who had guarded its length and breadth
for fifty years, vindictive, fiercely ravenous for blood,
soon realized that one of the race of men
was looking down into the monsters' lair.
Then she grasped him, clutched the Geat
in her ghastly claws; and yet she did not
so much as scratch his skin; his coat of mail
protected him; she could not penetrate
the linked metal rings with her loathsome fingers.
Then the sea-wolf dived to the bottom-most depths,
swept the prince to the place where she lived,
so that he, for all his courage, could not
wield a weapon; too many wondrous creatures
harassed him as he swam; many sea-serpents
with savage tusks tried to bore through his corslet,
the monsters molested him. Then the hero saw
that he had entered some loathsome hall
in which there was no water to impede him,
a vaulted chamber where the floodrush
could not touch him.* A light caught his eye,
a lurid flame flickering brightly.

Then the brave man saw the sea-monster,
fearsome, infernal; he whirled his blade,
swung his arm with all his strength,

and the ring-hilted sword sang a greedy war-song
on the monster's head. Then that guest realized
that his gleaming blade could not bite into her flesh,
break open her bone-chamber; its edge failed Beowulf
when he needed it; yet it had endured
many a combat, sheared often through the helmet,
split the corslet of a fated man; for the first time
that precious sword failed to live up to its name.*

Then, resolute, Hygelac's kinsman took his courage
in both hands, trusted in his own strength.
Angrily the warrior hurled Hrunting away,
the damascened sword with serpent patterns on its hilt;
tempered and steel-edged, it lay useless on the earth.
Beowulf trusted in his own strength,
the might of his hand. So must any man
who hopes to gain long-lasting fame
in battle; he must risk his life, regardless.
Then the prince of the Geats seized the shoulder
of Grendel's mother—he did not mourn their feud;
when they grappled, that brave man in his fury
flung his mortal foe to the ground.
Quickly she came back at him, locked him
in clinches and clutched at him fearsomely.
Then the greatest of warriors stumbled and fell.
She dropped on her hall-guest, drew her dagger,
broad and gleaming; she wanted to avenge her son,
her only offspring. The woven corslet
that covered his shoulders saved Beowulf's life,
denied access to both point and edge.
Then the leader of the Geats, Ecgtheow's son,
would have died far under the wide earth

had not his corslet, his mighty chain-mail,
guarded him, and had not holy God
granted him victory; the wise Lord,
Ruler of the Heavens, settled the issue
easily after the hero had scrambled to his feet.

Then Beowulf saw among weapons an invincible sword
wrought by the giants, massive and double-edged,
the joy of many warriors; that sword was matchless,
well-tempered and adorned, forged in a finer age,
only it was so huge that no man but Beowulf
could hope to handle it in the quick of combat.*
Ferocious in battle, the defender of the Scyldings
grasped the ringed hilt, swung the ornamented sword
despairing of his life—he struck such a savage blow
that the sharp blade slashed through her neck,
smashed the vertebrae; it severed her head
from the fated body; she fell at his feet.
The sword was bloodstained; Beowulf rejoiced.

A light gleamed; the chamber was illumined
as if the sky's bright candle were shining
from heaven. Hygelac's thane inspected
the vaulted room, then walked round the walls,
fierce and resolute, holding the weapon firmly
by the hilt. The sword was not too large
for the hero's grasp, but he was eager to avenge
at once all Grendel's atrocities,
all the many visits the monster had inflicted
on the West-Danes—which began with the time
he slew Hrothgar's sleeping hearth-companions,
devoured fifteen of the Danish warriors
even as they slept, and carried off as many more,

a monstrous prize. But the resolute warrior
had already repaid him to such a degree
that he now saw Grendel lying on his death-bed,
his life's-blood drained because of the wound
he sustained in battle at Heorot. Then Grendel's corpse
received a savage blow at the hero's hands,
his body burst open: Beowulf lopped off his head.

    At once the wise men, anxiously gazing at
the lake with Hrothgar, saw that the water
had begun to chop and churn, that the waves
were stained with blood. The grey-haired Scyldings
discussed that bold man's fate, agreed
there was no hope of seeing that brave thane again—
no chance that he would come, rejoicing in victory,
before their renowned king; it seemed certain
to all but a few that the sea-wolf had destroyed him.*

    Then the ninth hour came.* The noble Scyldings
left the headland; the gold-friend of men
returned to Heorot; the Geats, sick at heart,
sat down and stared at the lake.
Hopeless, they yet hoped to set eyes
on their dear lord.

              Then the battle-sword
began to melt like a gory icicle
because of the monster's blood. Indeed,
it was a miracle to see it thaw entirely,
as does ice when the Father (He who ordains
all times and seasons) breaks the bonds of frost,
unwinds the flood fetters; He is the true Lord.*
The leader of the Geats took none of the treasures
away from the chamber—though he saw many there—

except the monster's head and the gold-adorned
sword-hilt; the blade itself had melted,
the patterned sword had burnt, so hot was that blood,
so poisonous the monster who had died in the cave.
He who had survived the onslaught of his enemies
was soon on his way, swimming up through the water;
when the evil monster ended his days on earth,
left this transitory life, the troubled water
and all the lake's expanse was purged of its impurity.

Then the fearless leader of the seafarers
swam to the shore, exulting in his plunder,
the heavy burdens he had brought with him.
The intrepid band of thanes hurried towards him,
giving thanks to God, rejoicing
to see their lord safe and sound of limb.
The brave man was quickly relieved of his helmet
and corslet.
      The angry water under the clouds,
the lake stained with battle-blood, at last became calm.

Then they left the lake with songs on their lips,
retraced their steps along the winding paths
and narrow tracks; it was no easy matter
for those courageous men, bold as kings,
to carry the head away from the cliff
overlooking the lake. With utmost difficulty
four of the thanes bore Grendel's head
to the gold-hall on a battle-pole;
thus the fourteen Geats, unbroken
in spirit and eager in battle, very soon
drew near to Heorot; with them, that bravest
of brave men crossed the plain towards the mead-hall.

Then the fearless leader of the thanes,
covered with glory, matchless in battle,
once more entered Heorot to greet Hrothgar.
Grendel's head was carried by the hair
onto the floor where the warriors were drinking,
a ghastly thing paraded before the heroes and the queen.
Men stared at that wondrous spectacle.

Beowulf, the son of Ecgtheow, said:
'So, son of Healfdene, lord of the Scyldings,
we proudly lay before you plunder from the lake;
this head you look at proves our success.
I barely escaped with my life from that combat
under the water, the risk was enormous;
our encounter would have ended at once if God
had not guarded me. Mighty though it is,
Hrunting was no use at all in the battle;
but the Ruler of men—how often He guides
the friendless one—granted that I
should see a huge ancestral sword hanging,
shining, on the wall; I unsheathed it.
Then, at the time destiny decreed, I slew
the warden of the hall. And when the blood,
the boiling battle-blood burst from her body,
that sword burnt, the damascened blade
was destroyed. I deprived my enemies
of that hilt; I repaid them as they deserved
for their outrages, murderous slaughter of the Danes.
I promise, then, O prince of the Scyldings,
that you can sleep in Heorot without anxiety,
rest with your retainers, with all the thanes
among your people—experienced warriors

and striplings together—without further fear
of death's shadow skulking near the hall.'

Then the golden hilt, age-old work of giants,
was given to Hrothgar, the grizzled warrior,
the warlike lord; wrought by master-smiths,
it passed into the hands of the Danish prince
once the demons died; for that embittered fiend,
enemy of God, guilty of murder
had abandoned this world—and so had his mother.
Thus the hilt was possessed by the best
of earthly kings between the two seas,
the best of those who bestowed gold on Norse men.

Hrothgar spoke, first examining the hilt,
the ancient heirloom. On it was engraved
the origins of strife in time immemorial,
when the tide of rising water drowned
the race of giants; their end was horrible;
they were opposed to the Eternal Lord,
and their reward was the downpour and the flood.
Also, on the sword-guards of pure gold,
it was recorded in runic letters, as is the custom,
for whom that sword, finest of blades,
with twisted hilt and serpentine patterning
had first been made.*
                                    Then Healfdene's wise son
lifted his voice—everyone listened:
'This land's grizzled guardian, who promotes truth
and justice amongst his people, and forgets nothing
though the years pass, can say for certain that this man
is much favoured by fate! Beowulf my friend,
your name is echoed in every country

[ 56 ]

to earth's end. You wear your enormous might
with wisdom and with dignity. I shall keep
my promise made when last we spoke. You will
beyond doubt be the shield of the Geats
for days without number, and a source
of strength to warriors.
                              Heremod was hardly that
to Ecgwala's sons, the glorious Scyldings;*
he grew to spread slaughter and destruction
rather than happiness amongst the Danish people.
In mad rage he murdered his table-companions,
his most loyal followers; it came about
that the great prince cut himself off
from all earthly pleasures, though God had endowed him
with strength and power above all other men,
and had sustained him. For all that, his heart
was filled with savage blood-lust. He never gave
gifts to the Danes, to gain glory. He lived joyless,
agony racked him; he was long an affliction
to his people. Be warned, Beowulf,
learn the nature of nobility. I who tell you
this story am many winters old.
                              It is a miracle
how the mighty Lord in his generosity
gives wisdom and land and high estate
to people on earth; all things are in His power.
At times he allows a noble man's mind to experience
happiness, grants he should rule over a pleasant,
prosperous country, a stronghold of men,
makes subject to him regions of earth,
a wide kingdom, until in his stupidity

there is no end to his ambition.
His life is unruffled—neither old age
nor illness afflict him, no unhappiness
gnaws at his heart, in his land no hatred
flares up in mortal feuds, but all the world
bends to his will. He suffers no setbacks
until the seed of arrogance is sown and grows
within him, while still the watchman slumbers;
how deeply the soul's guardian sleeps
when a man is enmeshed in matters of this world;
the evil archer stands close with his drawn bow,
his bristling quiver. Then the poisoned shaft
pierces his mind under his helmet
and he does not know how to resist
the devil's insidious, secret temptations.
What had long contented him now seems insufficient;
he becomes embittered, begins to hoard
his treasures, never parts with gold rings
in ceremonial splendour; he soon forgets
his destiny and disregards the honours
given him of God, the Ruler of Glory.
In time his transient body wizens and withers,
and dies as fate decrees; then another man
succeeds to his throne who gives treasures and heirlooms
with great generosity; *he* is not obsessed with suspicions.
Arm yourself, dear Beowulf, best of men,
against such diseased thinking; always swallow pride;
remember, renowned warrior, what is more worthwhile—
gain everlasting. Today and tomorrow
you will be in your prime; but soon you will die,
in battle or in bed; either fire or water,

the fearsome elements, will embrace you,
or you will succumb to the sword's flashing edge,
or the arrow's flight, or terrible old age;
then your eyes, once bright, will be clouded over;
all too soon, O warrior, death will destroy you.

I have ruled the Ring-Danes under the skies
for fifty years, shielded them in war
from many tribes of men in this world,
from swords and from ash-spears, and the time had come
when I thought I had no enemies left on earth.
All was changed utterly, gladness
became grief, after Grendel,
my deadly adversary, invaded Heorot.
His visitations caused me continual pain.
Thus I thank the Creator, the Eternal Lord,
that after our afflictions I have lived to see,
to see with my own eyes this blood-stained head.
Now, Beowulf, brave in battle,
go to your seat and enjoy the feast;
tomorrow we shall share many treasures.'*

The Geat, full of joy, straightway went
to find his seat as Hrothgar had suggested.
Then, once again, as so often before,
a great feast was prepared for the brave warriors
sitting in the hall.

        The shadows of night
settled over the retainers. The company arose;
the grey-haired man, the old Scylding,
wanted to retire. And the Geat, the shield-warrior,
was utterly exhausted, his bones ached for sleep.
At once the chamberlain—he who courteously

saw to all such needs as a thane,
a travelling warrior, had in those days—
showed him, so limb-weary, to his lodging.

Then Beowulf rested; the building soared,
spacious and adorned with gold; the guest
slept within until the black raven gaily
proclaimed sunrise.* Bright light
chased away the shadows of night.

　　　　　　　　　　Then the warriors
hastened, the thanes were eager to return
to their own people; the brave seafarer
longed to see his ship, so far from that place.
Then the bold Geat ordered that Hrunting,
that sword beyond price, be brought before Unferth;
he begged him to take it back and thanked him
for the loan of it; he spoke of it as an ally
in battle, and assured Unferth he did not
underrate it: what a brave man he was!
After this the warriors, wearing their chain-mail,
were eager to be off; their leader,
so dear to the Danes, walked to the daïs
where Hrothgar was sitting, and greeted him.

Beowulf, the son of Ecgtheow, spoke:
'Now we seafarers, who have sailed here from far,
beg to tell you we are eager
to return to Hygelac. We have been happy here,
hospitably entertained; you have treated us kindly.
If I can in any way win more of your affection,
O ruler of men, than I have done already,
I will come at once, eager for combat.
If news reaches me over the seas

that you are threatened by those around you
(just as before enemies endangered you)
I will bring thousands of thanes,
all heroes, to help you. I know that Hygelac,
lord of the Geats, guardian of his people,
will advance me in word and deed
although he is young, so that I can back
these promises with spear-shafts, and serve you
with all my strength where you need men.
Should Hrethric, Hrothgar's son, wish
to visit the court of the Geatish king,
he will be warmly welcomed.* Strong men
should seek fame in far-off lands.'

Hrothgar replied: 'The wise Lord put these words
into your mind; I have never heard a warrior
speak more sagely while still so young.
You are very strong and very shrewd,
you speak with discerning. If your leader,
Hrethel's son, guardian of the people,
were to lose his life by illness or by iron,
by spear or grim swordplay, and if you survived him,
it seems to me that the Geats could not choose
a better man for king, should you wish to rule
the land of your kinsmen. Beloved Beowulf,
the longer I know you, the greater my regard for you.
Because of your exploit, your act of friendship,
there will be an end to the gross outrages,
the old enmity between Geats and Danes;
they will learn to live in peace.
For as long as I rule this spacious land,
heirlooms will be exchanged; many men

will greet their friends with gifts, send them
over the seas where gannets swoop and rise;
the ring-prowed ship will take tokens of esteem,
treasures across the waters. I know the Geats
are honourable to friend and foe alike,
always faithful to their ancient code.'
    Then Healfdene's son, guardian of thanes,
gave him twelve treasures in the hall,
told him to go safely with those gifts
to his own dear kinsmen, and to come back soon.
That king, descendant of kings,
leader of the Scyldings, kissed and embraced
the best of thanes; tears streamed down
the old man's face. The more that warrior thought,
wise and old, the more it seemed
improbable that they would meet again,
brave men in council. He so loved Beowulf
that he could not conceal his sense of loss;
but in his heart and in his head,
in his very blood, a deep love burned
for that dear man.
               Then Beowulf the warrior,
proudly adorned with gold, crossed the plain,
exulting in his treasure. The ship
rode at anchor, waiting for its owner.
Then, as they walked, they often praised
Hrothgar's generosity. He was an altogether
faultless king, until old age deprived him
of his strength, as it does most men.
    Then that troop of brave young retainers
came to the water's edge; they wore ring-mail,

woven corslets. And the same watchman
who had seen them arrive saw them now returning.
He did not insult them, ask for explanations,
but galloped from the cliff-top to greet the guests;
he said that those warriors in gleaming armour,
so eager to embark, would be welcomed home.
Then the spacious ship, with its curved prow,
standing ready on the shore, was laden with armour,
with horses and treasure. The mast towered
over Hrothgar's precious heirlooms.

Beowulf gave a sword bound round with gold
to the ship's watchman—a man who thereafter
was honoured on the mead-bench that much the more
on account of this heirloom.

The ship surged forward,
butted the waves in deep waters;
it drew away from the shores of the Scyldings.
Then a sail, a great sea-garment, was fastened
with guys to the mast; the timbers groaned;
the boat was not blown off its course
by the stiff sea-breezes. The ship swept
over the waves; foaming at the bows,
the boat with its well-wrought prow sped
over the waters, until at last the Geats
set eyes on the cliffs of their own country,
the familiar headlands; the vessel pressed forward,
pursued by the wind—it ran up onto dry land.

The harbour guardian hurried down to the shore;
for many days he had scanned the horizon,
anxious to see those dear warriors once more.
He tethered the spacious sea-steed with ropes

(it rode on its painter restlessly)
so that the rolling waves could not wrench it away.
Then Beowulf commanded that the peerless treasures,
the jewels and plated gold, be carried up from the shore.
He had not to go far to find the treasure-giver,
Hygelac, son of Hrethel, for his house and the hall
for his companions stood quite close to the sea-wall.
That high hall was a handsome building;
it became the valiant king.

Hygd, his queen,
Hæreth's daughter, was very young; but she
was discerning, and versed in courtly customs,
though she had lived a short time only
in that citadel; and she was not too thrifty,
not ungenerous with gifts of precious treasures
to the Geatish thanes.

Queen Thryth was proud
and perverse, pernicious to her people.
No hero but her husband, however bold,
dared by day so much as turn his head
in her direction—that was far too dangerous;
but, if he did, he could bargain on being cruelly
bound with hand-plaited ropes; soon
after his seizure, the blade was brought into play,
the damascened sword to settle the issue,
to inflict death. It is not right for a queen,
compelling though her beauty, to behave like this,
for a peace-weaver to deprive a dear man of his life
because she fancies she has been insulted.
But Offa, Hemming's kinsman, put an end to that.
Ale-drinking men in the hall have said

that she was no longer perfidious to her people,
and committed no crimes, once she had been given,
adorned with gold, to that young warrior
of noble descent—once she had sailed,
at her father's command, to Offa's court
beyond the pale gold sea. After that,
reformed, she turned her life to good account;
renowned for virtue, she reigned with vision;
and she loved the lord of warriors in the high way
of love—he who was, as I have heard,
the best of all men, the mighty human race,
between the two seas.* Offa the brave
was widely esteemed both for his gifts
and his skill in battle; he ruled his land
wisely. He fathered Eomer, guardian
of thanes, who was Hemming's kinsman,
grandson of Garmund, a goliath in battle.

   Then Beowulf and his warrior band walked
across the sand, tramped over
the wide foreshore; the world's candle shone,
the sun hastening from the south. The men hurried too
when they were told that the guardian of thanes,
Ongentheow's slayer,* the excellent young king,
held court in the hall, distributing rings.
Hygelac was informed at once of Beowulf's arrival—
that the shield of warriors, his comrade in battle,
had come back alive to the fortified enclosure,
was heading for the hall unscathed after combat.
Space on the benches for Beowulf and his band
was hastily arranged, as Hygelac ordered.

   The guardian of thanes formally greeted

that loyal man; then they sat down—
the unfated hero opposite the king,
kinsman facing kinsman. Hæreth's daughter
carried mead-cups round the hall,
spoke kindly to the warriors, handed the stoups
of wine to the thanes. Hygelac began
to ask his companion courteous questions
in the high hall; he was anxious to hear
all that had happened to the seafaring Geats:
'Beloved Beowulf, tell me what became of you
after the day you so hurriedly decided
to do battle far from here over the salt waters,
to fight at Heorot. And were you able
to assuage the grief, the well-known sorrow
of glorious Hrothgar? Your undertaking
deeply troubled me; I despaired, dear Beowulf,
of your return. I pleaded with you
not on any account to provoke that monster,
but to let the South-Danes settle their feud
with Grendel themselves. God be praised
that I am permitted to see you safe and home.'
    Then Beowulf, the son of Ecgtheow, said:
'Half the world, lord Hygelac, had heard
of my encounter, my great combat
hand to hand with Grendel in that hall
where he had harrowed and long humiliated
the glorious Scyldings. I avenged it all;
none of Grendel's brood, however long
the last of that hateful race survives,
steeped in crime, has any cause to boast about
that dawn combat.

First of all,
I went to the ring-hall to greet Hrothgar;
once Healfdene's great son knew of my intentions,
he assigned me a seat beside his own sons.
Then there was revelry; never in my life,
under heaven's vault, have I seen men
happier in the mead-hall. From time to time
the famous queen, the peace-weaver,* walked across the floor,
exhorting the young warriors; often she gave
some man a twisted ring before returning to her seat.
At times Hrothgar's daughter, whom I heard
men call Freawaru, carried the ale-horn
right round the hall in front of that brave company,
offered that vessel adorned with precious metals
to the thirsty warriors.

              Young, and decorated
with gold ornaments, she is promised to Froda's noble son,
Ingeld of the Heathobards; that match was arranged
by the lord of the Scyldings, guardian of the kingdom;
he believes that it is an excellent plan
to use her as a peace-weaver to bury old antagonisms,
mortal feuds. But the deadly spear rarely sleeps
for long after a prince lies dead in the dust,
however exceptional the bride may be!

   For Ingeld, leader of the Heathobards, and all
his retainers will later be displeased when he
and Freawaru walk on the floor—man and wife—
and when Danish warriors are being entertained.
For the guests will gleam with Heathobard heirlooms,
iron-hard, adorned with rings,
precious possessions that had belonged

to their hosts' fathers for as long as they
could wield their weapons, until in the shield-play
they and their dear friends forfeited their lives.
Then, while men are drinking, an old
warrior will speak; a sword he has seen,
marvellously adorned, stirs his memory
of how Heathobards were slain by spears;
he seethes with fury; sad in his heart,
he begins to taunt a young Heathobard,
incites him to action with these words:

    'Do you not recognize that sword, my friend,
the sword your father, fully armed, bore into battle
that last time, when he was slain by Danes,
killed by brave Scyldings who carried the field
when Withergyld fell and many warriors beside him?
See how the son of one of those
who slew him struts about the hall;
he sports the sword; he crows about that slaughter,
and carries that heirloom which is yours by right!'
In this way, with acid words, he will endlessly
provoke him and rake up the past,
until the time will come when a Danish warrior,
Freawaru's thane, sleeps blood-stained,
slashed by the sword, punished by death
for the deeds of his father; and the Heathobard
will escape, well-acquainted with the country.
Then both sides will break the solemn oath
sworn by their leaders; and Ingeld will come
to hate the Scyldings, and his love for his wife
will no longer be the same after such anguish and grief.
Thus I have little faith in friendship with Heathobards;

they will fail to keep their side of the promise,
friendship with the Danes.

                I have digressed;
Grendel is my subject. Now you must hear,
O treasure-giver, what the outcome was
of that hand-to-hand encounter. When the jewel of heaven
had journeyed over the earth, the angry one,
the terrible night-prowler paid us a visit—
unscathed warriors watching over Heorot.
A fight awaited Hondscio, a horrible end
for that fated man; he was the first to fall;
Grendel tore that famous young retainer to bits
between his teeth, and swallowed the whole body
of that dear man, that girded warrior.
And even then that murderer, mindful of evil,
his mouth caked with blood, was not content
to leave the gold-hall empty-handed
but, famed for his strength, he tackled me,
gripped me with his outstretched hand.
A huge unearthly glove swung at his side,*
firmly secured with subtle straps;
it had been made with great ingenuity,
with devils' craft and dragons' skins.
Innocent as I was, the demon monster
meant to shove me in it, and many another
innocent besides; that was beyond him
after I leapt up, filled with fury.
It would take too long to tell you how I repaid
that enemy of men for all his outrages;
but there, my prince, I ennobled your people
with my deeds. Grendel escaped,

and lived a little longer; but he left
behind at Heorot his right hand; and, in utter
wretchedness, sank to the bottom of the lake.

The sun rose; we sat down together
to feast, then the leader of the Scyldings
paid a good price for the bloody battle,
gave me many a gold-plated treasure.
There was talk and song; the grey-haired Scylding
opened his immense hoard of memories;
now and then a happy warrior touched
the wooden harp, reciting some story,
mournful and true; at times the generous king
recalled in proper detail some strange incident;
and as the shadows lengthened, an aged thane,
cramped and rheumatic, raised his voice
time and again, lamenting his lost youth,
his prowess in battle; worn with winters,
his heart quickened to the call of the past.*

In these ways we relaxed agreeably
throughout the long day until darkness closed in,
another night for men. Then, in her grief,
bent on vengeance, Grendel's mother
hastened to the hall where death had lain
in wait for her son—the battle-hatred
of the Geats. The horrible harridan avenged
her offspring, slew a warrior brazenly.
Æschere, the wise old counsellor, lost
his life. And when morning came,
the Danes were unable to cremate him,
to place the body of that dear man
on the funeral pyre; for Grendel's mother

had carried it off in her gruesome grasp,
taken it under the mountain lake.
Of all the grievous sorrows Hrothgar
long sustained, none was more terrible.
Then the king in his anger called upon your name
and entreated me to risk my life,
to accomplish deeds of utmost daring
in the tumult of waves; he promised me rewards.
And so, as men now know all over the earth,
I found the grim guardian of the lake-bottom.
For a while we grappled; the water boiled
with blood; then in that battle-hall,
I lopped off Grendel's mother's head
with the mighty sword. I barely escaped
with my life; but I was not fated.

And afterwards the guardian of thanes,
Healfdene's son, gave me many treasures.
Thus the king observed excellent tradition:
in no wise did I feel unrewarded
for all my efforts, but Healfdene's son
offered me gifts of my own choosing;
gifts, O noble king, I wish now
to give to you in friendship. I still depend
entirely on your favours; I have few
close kinsmen but you, O Hygelac!'

Then Beowulf caused to be brought in
a standard bearing the image of a boar,
together with a helmet towering in battle,
a grey corslet, and a noble sword; he said:
'Hrothgar, the wise king, gave me
these trappings and purposely asked me

to tell you their history: he said that Heorogar,
lord of the Scyldings, long owned them.
He, Heorogar, did not endow his own brave son,
Heoroweard, with this armour, much as
he loved him.* Make good use of everything!'

I heard that four bays, apple-brown,
were brought into the hall after the armour—
swift as the wind, identical. Beowulf gave them
as he gave the treasures. So should a kinsman do,
and never weave nets with underhand subtlety
to ensnare others, never have designs
on a close comrade's life. His nephew,
brave in battle, was loyal to Hygelac;
each man was mindful of the other's pleasure.

I heard that he gave Hygd the collar,
the wondrous ornament with which Wealhtheow,
daughter of the prince, had presented him,
and gave her three horses also, graceful creatures
with brightly-coloured saddles; Hygd
wore that collar,* her breast was adorned.

Thus Ecgtheow's son, feared in combat,
confirmed his courage with noble deeds;
he lived a life of honour, he never slew
companions at the feast; savagery was
alien to him, but he, so brave in battle,
made the best use of those ample talents
with which God endowed him.

                                He had been despised
for a long while, for the Geats saw no spark
of bravery in him, nor did their king deem him
worthy of much attention on the mead-bench;
people thought that he was a sluggard,

a feeble princeling. How fate changed,
changed completely for that glorious man!*
    Then the guardian of thanes, the famous king,
ordered that Hrethel's gold-adorned heirloom
be brought in; no sword was so treasured
in all Geatland; he laid it in Beowulf's lap,
and gave him seven thousand hides of land,
a hall and princely throne. Both men
had inherited land and possessions
in that country; but the more spacious kingdom
had fallen to Hygelac, who was of higher rank.


    In later days, after much turmoil,
things happened in this way: when Hygelac lay dead
and murderous battle-blades had beaten down
the shield of his son Heardred,
and when the warlike Swedes, savage warriors,
had hunted him down amongst his glorious people,
attacked Hereric's nephew with hatred,
the great kingdom of the Geats passed
into Beowulf's hands.* He had ruled it well
for fifty winters—he was a wise king,
a grizzled guardian of the land—when, on dark nights,
a dragon began to terrify the Geats:*
he lived on a cliff, kept watch over a hoard
in a high stone barrow; below, there was
a secret path; a man strayed
into this barrow by chance, seized
some of the pagan treasures, stole drinking vessels.
At first the sleeping dragon was deceived
by the thief's skill, but afterwards he avenged

this theft of gleaming gold; people far and wide,
bands of retainers, became aware of his wrath.

That man did not intrude upon the hoard
deliberately, he who robbed the dragon;
but it was some slave, a wanderer in distress
escaping from men's anger who entered there,
seeking refuge. He stood guilty of some sin.
As soon as he peered in, the outsider
stiffened with horror. Unhappy as he was,
he stole the vessel, the precious cup.
There were countless heirlooms in that earth-cave,
the enormous legacy of a noble people,
ancient treasures which some man or other
had cautiously concealed there many years
before. Death laid claim to all that people
in days long past, and then that retainer
who outlived the rest, a gold-guardian
mourning his friends, expected the same fate—
thought he would enjoy those assembled heirlooms
a little while only. A newly-built barrow
stood ready on a headland which overlooked
the sea, protected by the hazards of access.
To this barrow the protector of rings brought the heirlooms,
the plated gold, all that part of the precious treasure
worthy of hoarding; then he spoke a few words:
'Hold now, O earth, since heroes could not,
these treasures owned by nobles! Indeed, strong men
first quarried them from you. Death in battle,
ghastly carnage, has claimed all my people—
men who once made merry in the hall
have laid down their lives; I have no one

for a bond of peace.* Then the hoard was raided
and plundered, and that unhappy man
was granted his prayer. His lord examined
the ancient work of smiths for the first time.

    There was conflict once more after the dragon
awoke; intrepid, he slid swiftly
along by the rock, and found the footprints
of the intruder; that man had skilfully
picked his way right past the dragon's head.
Thus he who is undoomed will easily survive
anguish and exile provided he enjoys
the grace of God. The warden of the hoard
prowled up and down, anxious to find
the man who had pillaged it while he slept.
Breathing fire and filled with fury,
he circled the outside of the earth mound
again and again; but there was no one
in that barren place; yet he exulted at the thought
of battle, bloody conflict; at times he wheeled back
into the barrow, hunting for the priceless heirloom.
He realized at once that one of the race of men
had discovered the gold, the glorious treasure.
Restlessly the dragon waited for darkness;
the guardian of the hoard was bursting with rage,
he meant to avenge the vessel's theft
with fire.

          Then daylight failed
as the dragon desired; he could no longer
confine himself to the cave but flew in a ball
of flame, burning for vengeance. The Geats
were filled with dread as he began his flight;

it swiftly ended in disaster for their lord.

Then the dragon began to breathe forth fire,
to burn fine buildings; flame tongues flickered,
terrifying men; the loathsome winged creature
meant to leave the whole place lifeless.
Everywhere the violence of the dragon, the venom
of that hostile one, was clearly to be seen—
how he had wrought havoc, hated and humiliated
the Geatish people. Then, before dawn, he rushed back
to his hidden lair and the treasure hoard.
He had girdled the Geats with fire,
with ravening flames; he relied on his own strength,
and on the barrow and the cliff; his trust played him false.

Then news of that terror was quickly brought
to Beowulf, that flames enveloped
his own hall, best of buildings,
and the gift-throne of the Geats. That good man
was choked with intolerable grief.
Wise that he was, he imagined
he must have angered God, the Lord Eternal,
by ignoring some ancient law; he was seldom
dispirited, but now his heart surged with dark fears.*

The fire dragon had destroyed the fortified hall,
the people's stronghold, and laid waste with flames
the land by the sea. The warlike king,
prince of the Geats, planned to avenge this.
The protector of warriors, leader of men,
instructed the smith to forge a curious shield
made entirely of iron; he well knew
that a linden shield would not last long
against the flames. The eminent prince

[ 77 ]

was doomed to reach the end of his days on earth,
his life in this world.* So too was the dragon,
though he had guarded the hoard for generations.

Then the giver of gold disdained
to track the dragon with a troop
of warlike men; he did not shrink
from single combat, nor did he set much store
by the fearless dragon's power, for had he not before
experienced danger, again and again
survived the storm of battle, beginning with that time
when, blessed with success, he cleansed
Hrothgar's hall, and crushed in battle
the monster and his vile mother?*

                                    That grim combat
in which Hygelac was slain—Hrethel's son,
leader of the Geats, dear lord of his people,
struck down by swords in the bloodbath
in Frisia—was far from the least
of his encounters. Beowulf escaped
because of his skill and stamina at swimming;
he waded into the water, bearing no fewer
than thirty corslets, a deadweight on his arms.
But the Frankish warriors who shouldered
their shields against him had no cause to boast
about that combat; a handful only
eluded that hero and returned home.
Then the son of Ecgtheow, saddened and alone,
rode with the white horses to his own people.
Hygd offered him heirlooms there, and even
the kingdom, the ancestral throne itself; for she feared
that her son would be unable to defend it

from foreign invaders now that Hygelac was gone.
But the Geats, for all their anguish, failed
to prevail upon the prince—he declined
absolutely to become Heardred's lord,
or to taste the pleasures of royal power.
But he stood at his right hand,
ready with advice, always friendly,
and respectful, until the boy came of age
and could rule the Geats himself.*

                                   Two exiles,
Ohthere's sons, sailed to Heardred's court;
they had rebelled against the ruler of the Swedes,
a renowned man, the best of sea-kings,
gold-givers in Sweden.* By receiving them,
Heardred rationed the days of his life;
in return for his hospitality, Hygelac's son
was mortally wounded, slashed by swords.
Once Heardred lay lifeless in the dust,
Onela, son of Ongentheow, sailed home again;
he allowed Beowulf to inherit the throne
and rule the Geats; he was a noble king!
But Beowulf did not fail with help
after the death of the prince, although years passed;
he befriended unhappy Eadgils, Ohthere's son,
and supplied him with weapons and warriors
beyond the wide seas. Eadgils afterwards
avenged Eanmund, he ravaged and savaged
the Swedes, and killed the king, Onela himself.

    Thus the son of Ecgtheow had survived
these feuds, these fearful battles, these acts
of single combat, up to that day

when he was destined to fight against the dragon.
Then in fury the leader of the Geats set out
with eleven to search for the winged serpent.
By then Beowulf knew the cause of the feud,
bane of men; the famous cup
had come to him through the hands of its finder.
The unfortunate slave who first brought about
such strife made the thirteenth man
in that company—cowed and disconsolate,
he had to be their guide. Much against his will,
he conducted them to the entrance of the cave,
an earth-hall full of filigree work
and fine adornments close by the sea,
the fretting waters. The vile guardian,
the serpent who had long lived under the earth,
watched over the gold, alert; he who hoped
to gain it bargained with his own life.
  Then the brave king sat on the headland,
the gold-friend of the Geats wished success
to his retainers. His mind was most mournful,
angry, eager for slaughter; fate hovered
over him, so soon to fall on that old man,
to seek out his hidden spirit, to split
life and body; flesh was to confine
the soul of the king only a little longer.
Beowulf, the son of Ecgtheow, spoke:
'Often and often in my youth I plunged
into the battle maelstrom; how well I remember it.
I was seven winters old when the treasure guardian,
ruler of men, received me from my father.
King Hrethel took me into his ward, reared me,

fed me, gave me gold, mindful of our kinship;
for as long as he lived, he loved me no less
than his own three sons, warriors with me
in the citadel, Herebeald, Hæthcyn, and my dear Hygelac.
A death-bed for the firstborn was unrolled
most undeservedly by the action of his kinsman—
Hæthcyn drew his horn-tipped bow
and killed his lord-to-be; he missed his mark,
his arrow was stained with his brother's blood.
That deed was a dark sin, sickening
to think of, not to be settled by payment of *wergild*;
yet Herebeald's death could not be requited.*
    In the same way, an old man grieves
to see his son, so young, swing
from the gallows.* He sings a dirge, a song
dark with sorrow, while his son hangs,
raven's carrion, and he cannot help him
in any way, wise and old as he is.
He wakes each dawn to the ache
of his son's death; he has no desire
for a second son, to be his heir
in the stronghold, now that his firstborn
has finished his days and deeds on earth.
Grieving, he wanders through his son's dwelling,
sees the wine-hall now deserted, joyless,
home of the winds; the riders, the warriors,
sleep in their graves. No longer is the harp
plucked, no longer is there happiness in that place.
So Hrethel takes to his bed, and intones
dirges for his dead son, Herebeald;
his house and his lands seem empty now,

and far too large. Thus the lord of the Geats
endured in his heart the ebb and flow
of sorrow for his firstborn; but he could not
avenge that feud on the slayer—his own son;
although Hrethel had no love for Hæthcyn,
he could no more readily requite death
with death. Such was his sorrow that he lost
all joy in life, chose the light of God;
he bequeathed to his sons, as a wealthy man does,
his citadel and land, when he left this life.

Then there was strife, savage conflict
between Swedes and Geats; after Hrethel's death
the feud we shared, the fierce hatred
flared up across the wide water.
The sons of Ongentheow, Onela and Ohthere,
were brave and battle-hungry; they had no wish
for peace over the sea but several times,
and wantonly, butchered the people of the Geats
on the slopes of Slaughter Hill. As is well known,
my kinsmen requited that hatred, those crimes;
but one of them paid with his own life—
a bitter bargain; that fight was fatal
to Hæthcyn, ruler of the Geats.
Then I heard that in the morning
one kinsman avenged another, repaid
Hæthcyn's slayer with the battle-blade,
when Ongentheow attacked the Geat Eofor;
the helmet split, the old Swede fell,
pale in death; Eofor remembered
that feud well enough, his hand and sword
spared nothing in their death-swing.

I repaid Hygelac for his gifts of heirlooms
with my gleaming blade, repaid him in battle,
as was granted to me; he gave me land
and property, a happy home. He had
no need to hunt out and hire mercenaries—
inferior warriors from the Gepidae,
from the Spear-Danes or from tribes in Sweden;
but I was always at the head of his host,
alone in the van; and I shall still fight
for as long as I live and this sword lasts,
that has often served me early and late
since I became the daring slayer
of Dæghrefn, champion of the Franks.
He was unable to bring adornments,
breast-decorations to the Frisian king,
but fell in the fight bearing the standard,
a brave warrior; it was my battle-grip,
not the sharp blade, that shattered his bones,
silenced his heartbeat.* Now the shining edge,
hand and tempered sword, shall engage in battle
for the treasure hoard. I fought many battles
when I was young; yet I will fight again,
the old guardian of my people, and achieve
a mighty exploit if the evil dragon dares
confront me, dares come out of the earth-cave!'
    Then he addressed each of the warriors,
the brave heroes, his dear companions,
a last time: 'I would not wield a sword
against the dragon if I could grasp this hideous being
with my hands (and thus make good my boast),
as once I grasped the monster Grendel;

but I anticipate blistering battle-fire,
venomous breath; therefore I have with me
my shield and corslet. I will not give an inch
to the guardian of the mound, but at that barrow
it will befall us both as fate ordains,
every man's master. My spirit is bold,
I will not boast further against the fierce flier.
Watch from the barrow, warriors in armour,
guarded by corslets, which of us will better
weather his wounds after the combat.
This is not your undertaking, nor is it
possible for any man but me alone
to pit his strength against the gruesome one,
and perform great deeds. I will gain the gold
by daring, or else battle, dread destroyer
of life, will lay claim to your lord.'
      Then the bold warrior, stern-faced beneath his helmet,
stood up with his shield; sure of his own strength,
he walked in his corslet towards the cliff;
the way of the coward is not thus!
Then that man endowed with noble qualities,
he who had braved countless battles, weathered
the thunder when warrior troops clashed together,
saw a stone arch set in the cliff
through which a stream spurted; steam rose
from the boiling water; he could not stay long
in the hollow near the hoard for fear
of being scorched by the dragon's flames.
Then, such was his fury, the leader of the Geats
threw out his chest and gave a great roar,
the brave man bellowed; his voice, renowned

in battle, hammered the grey rock's anvil.
The guardian of the hoard knew the voice for human;
violent hatred stirred within him. Now no time
remained to entreat for peace. At once
the monster's breath, burning battle vapour,
issued from the barrow; the earth itself snarled.
The lord of the Geats, standing under the cliff,
raised his shield against the fearsome stranger;
then that sinuous creature spoiled
for the fight. The brave and warlike king
had already drawn his keen-edged sword,
(it was an ancient heirloom); a terror of each other
lurked in the hearts of the two antagonists.
While the winged creature coiled himself up,
the friend and lord of men stood unflinching
by his shield; Beowulf waited ready armed.

Then, fiery and twisted, the dragon swiftly
shrithed towards its fate. The shield protected
the life and body of the famous prince
for far less time than he had looked for.
It was the first occasion in all his life
that fate did not decree triumph for him
in battle. The lord of the Geats raised
his arm, and struck the mottled monster
with his vast ancestral sword; but the bright blade's
edge was blunted by the bone, bit
less keenly than the desperate king required.
The defender of the barrow bristled with anger
at the blow, spouted murderous fire, so that flames
leaped through the air. The gold-friend of the Geats
did not boast of famous victories; his proven sword,

the blade bared in battle, had failed him
as it ought not to have done. That great Ecgtheow's
greater son had to journey on from this world
was no pleasant matter; much against his will,
he was obliged to make his dwelling
elsewhere—sooner or later every man must leave
this transitory life. It was not long
before the fearsome ones closed again.
The guardian of the hoard was filled with fresh hope,
his breast was heaving; he who had ruled a nation
suffered agony, surrounded by flame.
And Beowulf's companions, sons of nobles—
so far from protecting him in a troop together,
unflinching in the fight—shrank back into the forest
scared for their own lives.* One man alone
obeyed his conscience. The claims of kinship
can never be ignored by a right-minded man.

His name was Wiglaf, a noble warrior,
Weohstan's son, kinsman of Ælfhere,
a leader of the Swedes; he saw that his lord,
helmeted, was tormented by the intense heat.
Then he recalled the honours Beowulf had bestowed
on him—the wealthy citadel of the Wægmundings,
the rights to land his father owned before him.
He could not hold back then; he grasped the round,
yellow shield; he drew his ancient sword,
reputed to be the legacy of Eanmund,
Ohthere's son.*
                    Weohstan had slain him
in a skirmish while Eanmund was a wanderer,
a friendless man, and then had carried off

to his own kinsmen the gleaming helmet,
the linked corslet, the ancient sword
forged by giants. It was Onela,
Eanmund's uncle, who gave him that armour,
ready for use; but Onela did not refer to the feud,
though Weohstan had slain his brother's son.*
For many years Weohstan owned that war-gear,
sword and corslet, until his son was old enough
to achieve great feats as he himself had done.
Then, when Weohstan journeyed on from the earth,
an old man, he left Wiglaf—who was
with the Geats—a great legacy of armour
of every kind.
                              This was the first time
the young warrior had weathered the battle storm,
standing at the shoulder of his lord.
His courage did not melt, nor did his kinsman's sword
fail him in the fight. The dragon found that out
when they met in mortal combat.

   Wiglaf spoke, constantly reminding
his companions of their duty—he was mournful.
'I think of that evening we emptied the mead-cup
in the feasting-hall, partook and pledged our lord,
who presented us with rings, that we would repay him
for his gifts of armour, helmets and hard swords,
if ever the need, need such as this, arose.
For this very reason he asked us
to join with him in this journey, deemed us
worthy of renown, and gave me these treasures;
he looked on us as loyal warriors,
brave in battle; even so, our lord,

guardian of the Geats, intended to perform
this feat alone, because of all men
he had achieved the greatest exploits,
daring deeds. Now the day has come
when our lord needs support, the might
of strong men; let us hurry forward
and help our leader as long as fire remains,
fearsome, searing flames. God knows
I would rather that fire embraced my body
beside the charred body of my gold-giver;
it seems wrong to me that we should shoulder
our shields, carry them home afterwards,
unless we can first kill the venomous foe,
guard the prince of the Geats. I know
in my heart his feats of old were such
that he should not now be the only Geat to suffer
and fall in combat; in common we shall share
sword, helmet, corslet, the trappings of war.'*

Then that man fought his way through the fumes,
went helmeted to help his lord. He shouted out:
'Brave Beowulf, may success attend you—
for in the days when you were young, you swore
that so long as you lived you would never allow
your fame to decay; now, O resolute king,
renowned for your exploits, you must guard your life
with all your skill. I shall assist you.'

At this the seething dragon attacked a second time;
shimmering with fire the venomous visitor fell on his foes,
the men he loathed. With waves of flame, he burnt
the shield right up to its boss; Wiglaf's
corslet afforded him no protection whatsoever.

But the young warrior still fought bravely, sheltered
behind his kinsman's shield after his own
was consumed by flames. Still the battle-king
set his mind on deeds of glory; with prodigious strength
he struck a blow so violent that his sword stuck
in the dragon's skull. But Nægling snapped!
Beowulf's old grey-hued sword
failed him in the fight. Fate did not ordain
that the iron edge should assist him
in that struggle; Beowulf's hand was too strong.
Indeed I have been told that he overtaxed
each and every weapon, hardened by blood, that he bore
into battle; his own great strength betrayed him.
      Then the dangerous dragon, scourge of the Geats,
was intent a third time upon attack; he rushed
at the renowned man when he saw an opening:
fiery, battle-grim, he gripped the hero's neck
between his sharp teeth; Beowulf was bathed
in blood; it spurted out in streams.
Then, I have heard, the loyal thane
alongside the Geatish king displayed great courage,
strength and daring, as was his nature.
To assist his kinsman, that man in mail
aimed not for the head but lunged at the belly
of their vile enemy (in so doing his hand
was badly burnt); his sword, gleaming and adorned,
sank in up to the hilt and at once the flames
began to abate. The king still had control then
over his senses; he drew the deadly knife,
keen-edged in battle, that he wore on his corslet;
then the lord of the Geats dispatched the dragon.

Thus they had killed their enemy—their courage
enabled them—the brave kinsmen together
had destroyed him. Such should a man,
a thane, be in time of necessity!

                              That was the last
of all the king's achievements, his last
exploit in the world. Then the wound
the earth-dragon had inflicted with his teeth
began to burn and swell; very soon he
was suffering intolerable pain as the poison
boiled within him. Then the wise leader
tottered forward and slumped on a seat
by the barrow; he gazed at the work of giants,
saw how the ancient earthwork contained
stone arches supported by columns.
Then, with his own hands, the best of thanes
refreshed the renowned prince with water,
washed his friend and lord, blood-stained
and battle-weary, and unfastened his helmet.

  Beowulf began to speak, he defied
his mortal injury; he was well aware
that his life's course, with all its delights,
had come to an end; his days on earth
were exhausted, death drew very close:
'It would have made me happy, at this time,
to pass on war-gear to my son, had I
been granted an heir to succeed me,
sprung of my seed. I have ruled the Geats
for fifty winters; no king of any
neighbouring tribe has dared to attack me
with swords, or sought to cow and subdue me.

But in my own home I have awaited
my destiny, cared well for my dependants,
and I have not sought trouble, or sworn
any oaths unjustly. Because of all these things
I can rejoice, drained now by death-wounds;
for the Ruler of Men will have no cause to blame me
after I have died on the count that I deprived
other kinsmen of their lives. Now hurry,
dear Wiglaf; rummage the hoard
under the grey rock, for the dragon sleeps,
riddled with wounds, robbed of his treasure.
Be as quick as you can so that I may see
the age-old store of gold, and examine
all the priceless, shimmering stones; once I
have set eyes on such a store, it will be
more easy for me to die, to abandon
the life and land that have so long been mine.'

   Then, I have been told, as soon as he heard
the words of his lord, wounded in battle,
Wiglaf hastened into the earth-cavern,
still wearing his corslet, his woven coat of mail.
After the fierce warrior, flushed with victory,
had walked past a daïs, he came upon
the hoard—a hillock of precious stones,
and gold treasure glowing on the ground;
he saw wondrous wall-hangings; the lair
of the serpent, the aged twilight-flier;
and the stoups and vessels of a people
long dead, now lacking a polisher,
deprived of adornments. There were many old,
rusty helmets, and many an armlet

cunningly wrought. A treasure hoard,
gold in the ground, will survive its owner
easily, whosoever hides it!
And he saw also hanging high
over the hoard a standard fashioned with gold strands,
a miracle of handiwork; a light shone from it,
by which he was able to distinguish the earth
and look at the adornments. There was no sign
of the serpent, the sword had ravaged and slain him.
Then I heard that Wiglaf rifled the hoard
in the barrow, the antique work of giants—
he chose and carried off as many cups and salvers
as he could; and he also took the standard,
the incomparable banner; Beowulf's sword,
iron-edged, had injured
the guardian of the hoard, he who had held it
through the ages and fought to defend it
with flames—terrifying, blistering,
ravening at midnight—until he was slain.
Wiglaf hurried on his errand, eager to return,
spurred on by the treasures; in his heart he was troubled
whether he would find the prince of the Geats,
so grievously wounded, still alive
in the place where he had left him.
Then at last he came, carrying the treasures,
to the renowned king; his lord's life-blood
was ebbing; once more he splashed him
with water, until Beowulf revived a little,
began to frame his thoughts.

            Gazing at the gold,
the warrior, the sorrowing king, said:

'With these words I thank
the King of Glory, the Eternal Lord,
the Ruler, for all the treasures here before me,
that in my lifetime I have been able
to gain them for the Geats.
And now that I have bartered my old life
for this treasure hoard, you must serve
and inspire our people. I will not long be with you.
Command the battle-warriors, after the funeral fire,
to build a fine barrow overlooking the sea;
let it tower high on Whaleness
as a reminder to my people.
And let it be known as *Beowulf's barrow*
to all seafarers, to men who steer their ships
from far over the swell and the saltspray.'*

Then the prince, bold of mind, detached
his golden collar and gave it to Wiglaf,
the young spear-warrior, and also his helmet
adorned with gold, his ring and his corslet,
and enjoined him to use them well;
'You are the last survivor of our family,
the Wægmundings;* fate has swept
all my kinsmen, those courageous warriors,
to their doom. I must follow them.'

Those were the warrior's last words
before he succumbed to the raging flames
on the pyre; his soul migrated from his breast
to meet the judgement of righteous men.

Then it was harrowing for the young hero
that he should have to see that beloved man
lying on the earth at his life's end,

wracked by pain. His slayer lay
there too, himself slain, the terrible
cave-dragon.\* That serpent, coiled evilly,
could no longer guard the gold-hoard,
but blades of iron, beaten and tempered
by smiths, notched in battle, had taken him off;
his wings were clipped now, he lay
mortally wounded, motionless on the earth
at the mound's entrance. No more did he fly
through the night sky, or spread his wings,
proud of his possessions,\* but he lay prostrate
because of the power of Beowulf, their leader.
Truly, I have heard that no hero of the Geats,
no fire-eater, however daring, could quell
the scorching blast of that venomous one
and lay his hands on the hoard in the lair,
should he find its sentinel waiting there,
watching over the barrow. Beowulf paid
the price of death for that mighty hoard;
both he and the dragon had travelled to the end
of this transitory life.
     Not long after that
the lily-livered ones slunk out of the wood;
ten cowardly oath-breakers, who had lacked
the courage to let fly with their spears
as their lord so needed, came forward together;
overcome with shame, they carried their shields
and weapons to where their leader lay;
they gazed at Wiglaf. That warrior, bone-weary,
knelt beside the shoulders of his lord; he tried
to rouse him with water; it was all in vain.

For all his efforts, his longing, he could not
detain the life of his leader on earth,
or alter anything the Ruler ordained.
God in His wisdom governed the deeds
of all men, as He does now.

    Then the young warrior was not at a loss
for well-earned, angry words for those cowards.
Wiglaf, Weohstan's son, sick at heart,
eyed those faithless men and said:
'He who does not wish to disguise the truth
can indeed say that—when it was a question
not of words but war—our lord completely wasted
the treasures he gave you, the same war-gear
you stand in over there, helmets and corslets
the prince presented often to his thanes on the ale-bench
in the feasting-hall, the very finest weapons
he could secure from far and wide.
The king of the Geats had no need to bother
with boasts about his battle-companions;
yet God, Giver of victories, granted
that he should avenge himself with his sword
single-handed, when all his courage was called for.
I could hardly begin to guard his life
in the fight; but all the same I attempted
to help my kinsman beyond my power.
Each time I slashed at that deadly enemy,
he was a little weaker, the flames leaped
less fiercely from his jaws. Too few defenders
rallied round our prince when he was most pressed.
Now you and your dependants can no longer delight
in gifts of swords, or take pleasure in property,

a happy home; but, after thanes from far and wide
have heard of your flight, your shameful cowardice,
each of your male kinsmen will be condemned
to become a wanderer, an exile deprived
of the land he owns. For every warrior
death is better than dark days of disgrace.'

Then Wiglaf ordered that Beowulf's great feat
be proclaimed in the stronghold, up along the cliff-edge,
where a troop of shield-warriors had waited all morning,
wondering sadly if their dear lord was dead,
or if he would return.

               The man who galloped
to the headland gave them the news at once;
he kept back nothing but called out:
'The lord of the Geats, he who gave joy
to all our people, lies rigid on his death-bed;
slaughtered by the dragon, he now sleeps;
and his deadly enemy, slashed by the knife,
sleeps beside him; he was quite unable
to wound the serpent with a sword. Wiglaf,
son of Weohstan, sits by Beowulf,
the quick and the dead—both brave men—
side by side; weary in his heart
he watches over friend and foe alike.

Now the Geats must make ready for a time
of war, for the Franks and the Frisians,
in far-off regions, will hear soon
of the king's death. Our feud with the Franks
grew worse when Hygelac sailed with his fleet
to the shores of Frisia. Frankish warriors
attacked him there, and outfought him,

bravely forced the king in his corslet
to give ground; he fell, surrounded
by his retainers; that prince presented
not one ornament to his followers. Since then,
the king of the Franks has been no friend of ours.

Nor would I in the least rely on peace
or honesty from the Swedish people; everyone
remembers how Ongentheow slew Hæthcyn,
Hrethel's son, in battle near Ravenswood
when, rashly, the Geats first attacked the Swedes.
At once Ongentheow, Ohthere's father,
old but formidable, retaliated; he killed
Hæthcyn, and released his wife from captivity,
set free the mother of Onela and Ohthere,
an aged woman bereft of all her ornaments;
and then he pursued his mortal enemies
until, lordless, with utmost difficulty,
they reached and found refuge in Ravenswood.*
Then Ongentheow, with a huge army, penned in
those warriors, exhausted by wounds,
who had escaped the sword; all night long
he shouted fearsome threats at those shivering thanes,
swore that in the morning he and his men would let
their blood in streams with sharp-edged swords,
and string some up on gallows-trees
as sport for birds.* Just as day dawned
those despairing men were afforded relief;
they heard the joyful song of Hygelac's
horn and trumpet as that hero came,
hurrying to their rescue with a band of retainers.
After that savage, running battle, the soil

was blood-stained, scuffled—a sign of how
the Swedes and the Geats fomented their feud.
Then Ongentheow, old and heavy-hearted,
headed for his stronghold with his retainers,
that resolute man retreated; he realized
how spirit and skill combined in the person
of proud Hygelac; he had no confidence
about the outcome of an open fight with the seafarers,
the Geatish warriors, in defence of his hoard,
his wife and children; the old man thus withdrew
behind an earth-wall. Then the Swedes were pursued,
Hygelac's banner was hoisted over that earth-work
after the Geats, sons of Hrethel, had stormed
the stronghold. Then grey-haired Ongentheow
was cornered by swords, the king of the Swedes
was constrained to face and suffer his fate
as Eofor willed it.* Wulf, the son
of Wonred, slashed angrily at Ongentheow
with his sword, so that blood spurted
from the veins under his hair. The old Swede,
king of his people, was not afraid
but as soon as he had regained his balance
repaid that murderous blow with interest.
Then Wonred's daring son could no longer
lift his hand against the aged warrior
but, with that stroke, Ongentheow had sheared
right through his helmet so that Wulf, blood-stained,
was thrown to the ground; he was not yet doomed to die
but later recovered from that grievous wound.
When Wulf collapsed, his brother Eofor,
Hygelac's brave thane, swung his broad sword,

made by giants, shattered the massive helmet
above the raised shield; Ongentheow fell,
the guardian of the people was fatally wounded.
Then many warriors quickly rescued Wulf,
and bandaged his wounds, once they had won control
(as fate decreed) of that field of corpses.
Meanwhile Eofor stripped Ongentheow's body
of its iron corslet, wrenched the helmet
from his head, the mighty sword from his hands;
he carried the old man's armour to Hygelac.
He received those battle adornments, honourably
promised to reward Eofor above other men;
he kept his word; the king of the Geats,
Hrethel's son, repaid Eofor and Wulf
for all they had accomplished with outstanding gifts
when he had returned home; he gave each of them
land and interlocked rings to the value
of a hundred thousand pence—no man on earth
had cause to blame the brothers for accepting
such wealth, they had earned it by sheer audacity.
Then, as a pledge of friendship, Hygelac gave
Eofor his only daughter to grace his home.

    That is the history of hatred and feud
and deadly enmity; and because of it,
I expect the Swedes to attack us
as soon as they hear our lord is lifeless—
he who in earlier days defended a land
and its treasure against two monstrous enemies
after the death of its heroes, daring Scyldings,
he who protected the people, and achieved feats
all but impossible.

Let us lose no time now
but go and gaze there upon our king
and carry him, who gave us rings,
to the funeral pyre. And let us not grudge gold
to melt with that bold man, for we have a mighty hoard,
a mint of precious metal, bought with pain;
and now, from this last exploit, a harvest
he paid for with his own life; these the fire
shall devour, the ravening flames embrace.
No thane shall wear or carry these treasures
in his memory, no fair maiden shall hang
an ornament of interlinked rings at her throat,
but often and again, desolate, deprived of gold,
they must tread the paths of exile,
now that their lord has laid aside laughter,
festivity, happiness. Henceforth, fingers must grasp,
hands must hold, many a spear
chill with the cold of morning; no sound of the harp
shall rouse the warriors but, craving for carrion,
the dark raven shall have its say
and tell the eagle how it fared at the feast
when, competing with the wolf, it laid bare the bones of
     corpses.'

Thus the brave messenger told of and foretold
harrowing times; and he was not far wrong.
Those events were fated. Every man in the troop
stood up, stained with tears, and set out
for Eagleness to see that strange spectacle.
There they found him lifeless on the sand,
the soft bed where he slept, who often before
had given them rings; that good man's days

on earth were ended; the warrior-king,
lord of the Geats, had died a wondrous death.
But first they saw a strange creature
there, a loathsome serpent lying
nearby; the fire-dragon, fierce
and mottled, was scorched by its own flames.
It measured fifty paces from head to tail;
sometimes it had soared at night
through the cool air, then dived
to its dark lair; now it lay rigid in death,
no longer to haunt caverns under the earth.
Goblets and vessels stood by it,
salvers and valuable swords, eaten through
by rust, as if they had lain
for a thousand winters in the earth's embrace.
That mighty legacy, gold of men long dead,
lay under a curse;* it was enchanted
so that no human might enter
the cavern save him to whom God,
the true Giver of Victories, Guardian of Men,
granted permission to plunder the hoard—
whichever warrior seemed worthy to Him.

Then it was clear that, whoever devised it,
the evil scheme of hiding the hoard under the rock
had come to nothing; the guardian had killed
a brave and famous man; that feud
was violently avenged. The day that a warrior,
renowned for his courage, will reach the end
(as fate ordains) of his life on earth,
that hour when a man may feast in the hall
with his friends no longer, is always unpredictable.

It was thus with Beowulf when he tracked down
and attacked the barrow's guardian; he himself
was not aware how he would leave this world.
The glorious princes who first placed that gold there
had solemnly pronounced that until domesday
any man attempting to plunder the hoard
should be guilty of wickedness, confined,
tormented and tortured by the devil himself.
Never before had Beowulf been granted
such a wealth of gold by the gracious Lord.

    Wiglaf, the son of Weohstan, said:
'Many thanes must often suffer
because of the will of one, as we do now.
We could not dissuade the king we loved,
or in any way restrain the lord of our land
from not drawing his sword against the gold-warden,
from not letting him lie where he had long lain
and remain in his lair until the world's end;
but he fulfilled his high destiny. The hoard,
so grimly gained, is now easy of access;
our king was driven there by too harsh a fate.
I took the path under the earth-wall,
entered the hall and examined all
the treasures after the dragon deserted it;
I was hardly invited there. Hurriedly
I grasped as many treasures as I could,
a huge burden, and carried them here
to my king; he was still alive then,
conscious and aware of this world around him.
He found words for his thronging thoughts,
born of sorrow, he asked me to salute you,

said that as a monument to your lord's exploits
you should build a great and glorious barrow
over his pyre, for he of all men
was the most famous warrior on the wide earth
for as long as he lived, happy in his stronghold.
Now let us hurry once more together
and see the hoard of priceless stones,
that wonder under the wall; I will lead you
so that you will come sufficiently close
to the rings, the solid gold. After we
get back, let us quickly build the bier,
and then let us carry our king,
the man we loved, to where he must
long remain in the Lord's protection.'

   Then the brave warrior, Weohstan's son,
directed that orders be given to many men
(to all who owned houses, elders of the people)
to fetch wood from far to place beneath
their prince on the funeral pyre:

                    'Now flames,
the blazing fire, must devour the lord of warriors
who often endured the iron-tipped arrow-shower,
when the dark cloud loosed by bow strings
broke above the shield-wall, quivering;
when the eager shaft, with its feather garb,
discharged its duty to the barb.'

   I have heard that Weohstan's wise son
summoned from Beowulf's band his seven
best thanes, and went with those warriors
into the evil grotto; the man leading
the way grasped a brand. Then those retainers

were not hesitant about rifling the hoard
as soon as they set eyes on any part of it,
lying unguarded, gradually rusting,
in that rock cavern; no man was conscience-stricken
about carrying out those priceless treasures
as quickly as he could. Also, they pushed the dragon,
the serpent over the precipice; they let the waves take him,
the dark waters embrace the warden of the hoard.
Then the wagon was laden with twisted gold,
with treasures of every kind, and the king,
the old battle-warrior, was borne to Whaleness.

Then, on the headland, the Geats prepared a mighty pyre
for Beowulf, hung round with helmets and shields
and shining mail, in accordance with his wishes;
and then the mourning warriors laid
their dear lord, the famous prince, upon it.

And there on Whaleness, the heroes kindled
the most mighty of pyres; the dark wood-smoke
soared over the fire, the roaring flames
mingled with weeping—the winds' tumult subsided—
until the body became ash, consumed even
to its core. The heart's cup overflowed;
they mourned their loss, the death of their lord.
And, likewise, a maiden of the Geats,
with her tresses swept up, intoned
a dirge for Beowulf time after time,
declared she lived in dread of days to come
dark with carnage and keening, terror of the enemy,
humiliation and captivity.

                   Heaven swallowed the smoke.
Then the Geats built a barrow on the headland—

it was high and broad, visible from far
to all seafarers; in ten days they built the beacon
for that courageous man; and they constructed
as noble an enclosure as wise men
could devise, to enshrine the ashes.
They buried rings and brooches in the barrow,
all those adornments that brave men
had brought out from the hoard after Beowulf died.
They bequeathed the gleaming gold, treasure of men,
to the earth, and there it still remains
as useless to men as it was before.

   Then twelve brave warriors, sons of heroes,
rode round the barrow, sorrowing;
they mourned their king, chanted
an elegy, spoke about that great man:
they exalted his heroic life, lauded
his daring deeds; it is fitting for a man,
when his lord and friend must leave this life,
to mouth words in his praise
and to cherish his memory.
Thus the Geats, his hearth-companions,
grieved over the death of their lord;
they said that of all kings on earth
he was the kindest, the most gentle,
the most just to his people, the most eager for fame.

# THE FIGHT AT FINNSBURH

... 'gables burning.'
Then Hnæf the king, a novice in battle, said:
'This is not dawn from the east, no dragon
flies here, the gables of the hall are not burning,
but men are making an attack. Birds of battle screech,
the grey wolf howls, spears rattle,
shield answers shaft. The wandering moon gleams
under the clouds; evil deeds will now
arise from this enmity of people.*
But rouse yourselves now, my warriors!
Grasp your shields, steel yourselves,
fight at the front and be brave!'
Then many a thane, laden in gold, buckled his sword-belt.
Then the stout warriors, Sigeferth and Eaha,
went to one door and unsheathed their swords;
Ordlaf and Guthlaf went to guard the other,
and Hengest himself followed in their footsteps.*
When he saw this, Guthere said to Garulf
that he would be unwise to go to the hall doors
in the first rush, risking his noble life,
for fearless Sigeferth was set upon his death.*
But that daring man drowned the other voices
and demanded openly who held the door.
'I am Sigeferth, a prince of the Secgan
and a well-known warrior; I've braved many trials,
tough combats. Even now it is decreed

for you what you can expect of me here.'
Then the din of battle broke out in the hall;*
the hollow shield, body-guardian, was doomed to shatter
in bold men's hands; the hall floor boomed.
Then Garulf, the son of Guthlaf,* gave his life
in the fight, first of all the warriors
living in that land, and many heroes fell around him,
the corpses of brave men. The raven wheeled,
dusky, dark brown. The gleaming swords so shone
it seemed as if all Finnsburh were in flames.*
I have never heard of sixty warriors, unbowed,
who bore themselves more bravely in the fight
and never did retainers better repay
glowing mead than those men repaid Hnæf.
They fought five days and not one of the followers
fell, but they held the doors firmly.
Then a warrior withdrew, a wounded man;
he said that his armour was almost useless,
his corselet broken, his helmet burst open.
The guardian of those people asked him at once
how well the warriors had survived their wounds*
or which of the young men. . . .

# EXPLANATORY NOTES

## BEOWULF

2  *Scyld Scefing*: the eponymous founder of the royal Danish house, the Scyldings. 'Scefing' probably means 'son of Scef', although if, as the poem tells us, he arrived miraculously from nowhere to save the Danish nation, set adrift in a boat like Moses in the bulrushes, it is perhaps surprising that his father should be commemorated in his name. A tenth-century Anglo-Saxon chronicle traces the genealogy of the kings of Anglo-Saxon Wessex (King Alfred's line) back to Scef, the father of Scyld; this Scef is said to arrive unknown, by boat, at a land called Scani, rather as Scyld does here. 'Scefing' could also mean 'of the sheaf', and a later, twelfth-century English chronicle tells the story of Sceldius, the son of Scef, who was driven ashore on an island called Scandza with a sheaf of corn lying beside him in the oarless boat; 'for this reason he was given the name Sceaf'. The two name elements, 'scyld' and 'sceaf', shield and sheaf, together represent the two most important aspects of early kingship—defence of the realm and a fruitful harvest each year. Whatever the relationship between the poem and these two chronicles, the founder of the Danes has an impressive and appealing mythic status. Old Norse historical tradition traces the Danish kings (the Skjöldungs) back to one Scioldus, the son of Odin, but neither *Skjöldunga saga* nor Saxo Grammaticus's *History of the Danes* mentions the boat or the sheaf of corn. (See G. N. Garmonsway and J. Simpson, *Beowulf and its Analogues* (London, 1968).)

*Beow*: the manuscript of the poem both here and at line 53 reads 'Beowulf'. It is conceivable that this early Danish king had the same name as the hero of the poem, but far more likely that the scribe wrote the name Beowulf by mistake, because the hero was uppermost in his mind. Anglo-Saxon genealogies record Beaw as the son of Scyld; it is also significant, given the sheaf connection, that 'beaw' is related to words for barley in Germanic languages.

3  *There in harbour . . . were gathered there*: archaeologists have excavated a number of ship burials in Britain and Scandinavia—most famously at Sutton Hoo, Oseberg, and Gokstad. The burial of a vehicle—a ship, in the grandest graves—is one of the standard features of the burials of aristocratic men in pagan Scandinavia. But Scyld Scefing is not buried with the ship; rather, his dead body, accompanied by treasures and war-gear, is sent out to sea in one, a practice which could, of course, hardly leave archaeological remains, but which does form a satisfying parallel to his mysterious arrival in

Denmark; see n. below. In the Latin Life of St Gildas, the dying saint gives instructions that his body should be set in a boat and its destination be left to God's providence, a remarkable parallel to Scyld, who has also decreed the form of his own funeral. (See A. Cameron, 'Saint Gildas and Scyld Scefing', *Neuphilologische Mitteilungen*, 70 (1969), 240–6.) St Gildas's end recalls the ascetic practice of Celtic monks, *peregrini*, who, in dedicating their lives to God, set off in oarless, rudderless boats as a dramatic gesture of absolute submission to God's will. Scyld's funeral, then, may combine a suggestion of pagan burial with an air of Christian asceticism.

*no less magnificent*: the treasure with which the Danes send off Scyld's body is in fact wonderfully more magnificent than that with which he arrived, since he came destitute to the Danes. This is a good example of understatement for rhetorical effect, popular in Old English poetry but oddsounding to modern readers.

*Mighty men . . . cannot say who received that cargo*: Scyld's arrival from and departure into the unknown recalls the famous story in Bede's *Ecclesiastical History* (II. 13), in which a crucial failure in pagan teaching is pointed out by reference to the simile of the sparrow in the mead-hall: the bird flies into the hall from a wintry outer darkness, has a few moments of light, warmth, and calm, and then flies out again into unknowable chaos. This is how human life appears to the pagan, while Christian teaching offers some understanding of an eternal context and a life after death. On a larger scale, the image may be said to reflect the shape and sense of the whole poem, which begins and ends with a funeral, its brightly lit characters playing their parts between unknown origins and a dark and dreaded future.

4 *Yrse . . . Swedish king*: the manuscript is defective here, and the name of Healfdene's daughter, and part of her husband's name, are missing. Old Norse sources link Yrse with the Danish royal house, and tell of her marriage to a Swedish king.

*The hall towered high . . . deeds of deadly enmity*: Hrothgar's daughter is to marry Ingeld, the son of Froda, a king of the Heathobards who have been at war with the Danes. The hope is that the alliance will heal the hostility between them. But Beowulf predicts later in the poem that the father-in-law (Hrothgar) and the son-in-law (Ingeld) will not be reconciled for long, and the warning here is that the feud will end with the burning down of Heorot. The feud is also referred to in the Old English poem *Widsith*, though there is no mention there of Heorot being destroyed by fire.

5 *He who could tell . . . base crimes*: the hall-poet's song about Creation is distinctly biblical in tone and diction (see especially Genesis 1: 2) and recalls Cædmon's *Hymn*, a brief Old English Creation poem quoted by Bede and celebrated as the first use of Old English poetic form for Christian

subject matter. These associations create the impression of Heorot as a kind of Eden, a paradise without sin or sorrow before Grendel appears.

5 *He could no longer . . . feel God's love*: in the original poem, these lines follow the poet's account of Grendel's terrifying occupation of Heorot (see p. 7). Bringing them forward to this point in the poem improves the coherence of the narrative.

*In him all evil-doers . . . their deserts*: that Cain was the ancestor of a race of monsters was a widespread medieval tradition, deriving from early commentaries on Genesis 4: 2 and 4, and from ancient Jewish writings such as the Book of Enoch. These monsters were often portrayed as cannibalistic giants, and some, according to tradition, survived the Flood to continue the race of Cain. (See R. Mellinkoff, 'Cain's Monstrous Progeny in *Beowulf*: Parts I and II', in *Anglo-Saxon England*, vols. 8 (1979) and 9 (1981).)

6 *hall-warden*: it is fiercely ironic to call Grendel Heorot's 'hall-warden', since, although he is a regular visitor to the hall, he does not guard it but in fact represents its greatest threat. The retainers who should guard the hall have been frightened off, leaving him as the only one to get gratification from the hall—not rings and praise, but freshly killed Danes to eat.

7 *wergild*: literally, 'man-payment', compensation for murder, paid to the victim's family as an alternative to a revenge killing.

*shrithe*: Crossley-Holland's own word, derived from the original Old English verb 'scriðan' and used throughout the poem for the terrifying and unnatural wanderings of Grendel and the dragon.

8 *they offered sacrifices . . . the glorious Ruler*: apart from this one reference, the poet makes no explicit mention of his characters' paganism, although he and his audience would have been quite clear that the Danes could not have been Christians. That Beowulf and Hrothgar make frequent pious reference to one Almighty God (and monotheism is not a characteristic of what we can piece together of Germanic paganism) and the identification of Grendel as a hellish monster give the impression that the Danes and Beowulf are natural allies of Christianity. The Danes' sacrifices disturb the elegant poise of the poem's ethical world, and even though the practice of dismissing explicitly Christian references in the poem as later interpolations has now gone out of fashion, some critics still feel that this passage does not belong to the 'original' poem. But idolatry is, in the Old Testament, a vice especially associated with the pre-Christian descendants of the righteous Noah.

10 *Warriors! . . . the cause of your coming*: the coastguard's confident challenge, and Beowulf's courteous reply, are in stark contrast to the account in the *Anglo-Saxon Chronicle* when in 787 an Anglo-Saxon official rode down to

the Dorset shore to greet a boatload of Scandinavians and was killed on the spot.

11 *The boar crest . . . grim warriors*: in Old Norse mythology, the boar was sacred to the god Freyr, and helmets decorated with boar images have been found in Britain and Scandinavia, for example at Sutton Hoo. Some helmets depict warriors wearing boar-crested helmets, and the poet may be imagining ancient war-gear rather than describing current fashions.

13 *You must have come . . . high ambition*: Beowulf's father, on the other hand, did come to Hrothgar as an exile—as the sons of Ohthere are said to take refuge with Hygelac's son, later in the poem.

*a prince of the Vandals*: Wulfgar's people may be the widely scattered tribe we know as Vandals, or may be Vendels, from North Jutland, known from *Widsith* as Wenlas.

16 *Weland*: like Daedalus and Vulcan in classical mythology, in Germanic tradition Weland was a celebrated smith, hamstrung and enslaved. As we learn (rather allusively) from the Old English poem *Deor*, Weland took revenge by seducing his captor's daughter and killing his two little sons; the story is vividly told in the Old Norse poem *Völundarkviða*, and depicted on one panel of the Franks Casket, an early eighth-century whalebone casket elaborately decorated with runes, and a mixture of Christian and Germanic iconography.

*Wylfings*: these may be the Wulfings mentioned in *Widsith*, and an attempt has been made to link them to the Wuffing dynasty in East Anglia alluded to by Bede. Ecgtheow and Heatholaf are not known elsewhere.

17 *Ecgtheow swore oaths to me*: the poet may mean either that Ecgtheow swore to keep the peace, or that he swore allegiance to Hrothgar.

18 *Unferth*: it has been suggested that Unferth's name, which may be translated as 'non-peace' ('strife'), or 'non-mind' ('folly'), is symbolic, reflecting Unferth's role and status in the poem (which is analogous to that of Laodamas in the *Odyssey*). The poet does not seem to use many symbolic names, but Beowulf (bee-wolf, or bear) and Wealhtheow (foreign slave) are both significant examples.

*Breca*: the name Breca is related to the Modern English word 'breaker', which has led some critics to read the contest as having its origins in a myth of a struggle against the elements. The nineteenth-century critic Karl Müllenhof saw the whole poem in these terms, identifying Beowulf's opponents as personifications of the destructive North Sea. This view is long outmoded, but it is suggestive that the name of Breca's tribe, the Brondings, relates to a Norwegian word for waves.

*shores of the Heathoreams*: since the Heathoreams lived in southern Norway, this would have been an epic contest indeed (Beowulf ends up in the land of the Lapps). Critics not happy with heroic overstatement have preferred to understand a (hardly more plausible) rowing contest.

19 *Are you the Beowulf . . . watches of the night*: such a hostile reception from Unferth (for which Hrothgar does not apologize, even though it contrasts so markedly with his own generous welcome to Beowulf) may be explained by reference to the Germanic tradition of *flyting*, in which a guest is verbally challenged and must prove his worth in return. (See Carol Clover, 'The Germanic Context of the Unferþ Episode', *Speculum*, 55 (1980), 444–68.)

20 *Truly . . . worn out by my venture*: Beowulf's own account of the contest has close parallels with his fight with Grendel's mother later on in the poem: hostile sea-creatures, protective armour, submission to fate, a light heralding victory, and eventual triumph. It also comprises one of the poem's several 'revised versions' of previously told material—for instance, Beowulf's re-telling of his reception at Heorot.

*you slew . . . your own close kinsmen*: Unferth as a fratricide is firmly linked to Cain, and thus by extension to Grendel and his mother. That Unferth is first pictured sitting at Hrothgar's feet may signify deep-seated trouble at the heart of the Danish court.

23 *It was said . . . a hall-guard*: it is of course God who has sent Beowulf to guard Heorot.

24 *Despite his fame . . . He should think fitting*: Grendel's subhuman status is reflected in his ignorance of weapons; Beowulf magnanimously refuses to take advantage of him. But there is a disturbing undercurrent to Beowulf's history of fighting without weapons: we learn much later in the poem that he crushes Dæghrefn to death in a bear-hug.

26 *so strong a grip*: the power of Beowulf's grip has already been commented on by Hrothgar.

27 *no man could wreck . . . greedy tongues of flame*: another oblique allusion to the eventual destruction of Heorot.

*no war-sword . . . battle-blade*: that Grendel turns out to be invulnerable to weapons reflects rather oddly on what Beowulf has said about his ignorance of them, but it does serve to explain why Beowulf's companions are not able to come to his aid.

28 *After that deadly encounter . . . accomplished*: there is a clear analogue to Beowulf's fight with Grendel in the later Old Norse *Grettir's saga*.

30 *Sigemund, the son of Wæls*: in the Old Norse version of this material (chiefly *Völsunga saga*—the story of the Volsungs—and some Eddaic poems) Sigmundr is the son of Völsungr (Wæls) but it is his son Siguðr who kills the dragon. Sigmundr sleeps with his sister Signý—thus ensuring no dilution of the family line—and their son is Sinfjötli, Fitela in Old

English. We cannot know for certain whether the *Beowulf* poet knew of this incestuous birth. Hrothgar's poet's recitation about Sigemund is usually believed to reflect flatteringly on Beowulf, setting him alongside the great heroes of Germanic legend and alluding proleptically to his own dragon fight. But it is also possible that Beowulf emerges from the comparison as a finer hero than the exile Sigemund (see n. to p. 13).

*he impaled . . . the dragon was slain*: according to *Völsunga saga* and the poetic sources on which it is based, Sigurðr kills the dragon Fafnir by digging a pit, crouching in it, and spearing the dragon's soft underbelly as the creature slithers its way to a water-hole. These differences in detail are especially significant in relation to the later account of Beowulf's own dragon fight, which is a bold confrontation rather than a cunning plan.

31  *Heremod's prowess . . . done to death*: at first, it seems that Heremod is introduced as one of Sigemund's illustrious predecessors, heroically killed fighting monsters. But the poet goes on to characterize Heremod as a notoriously bad king, who, unlike Beowulf, gets worse as he goes on. In Anglo-Saxon genealogies, Heremod precedes Scyld; perhaps we should see his disastrous reign as precipitating the Danes' leaderless crisis, from which Scyld rescues them. This brief passage may be seen as lying at the centre of a network of favourable and unfavourable comparisons between kings in the poem: there is also an implicit parallel to Hrothgar (who has failed to protect the Danes against Grendel, as Heremod also failed them) and an explicit comparison with Beowulf, 'loved by all who knew him'.

There is a parallel to Heremod's evil conduct in Saxo's *History*, attributed however to a figure called Hlotherus.

34  *after the banquet*: feasting in the hall is here a metaphor for life itself: the sleep after the feasting is a prefiguring of death. (See also n. to p. 3.)

*Heorot was packed . . . wrongful deeds*: this picture of conviviality is dramatically undermined by the reference to the future enmity amongst the Danes. Hrothgar and Hrothulf, uncle and nephew, seem to have a model relationship—as between Beowulf and Hygelac—but it is possible that the 'wrongful deeds' referred to by the poet indicate that Hrothulf will prove treacherous to Hrothgar.

*Hrothgar gave Beowulf . . . and a corslet*: one might have expected Hrothgar to hand his father's war-gear on to one of his own sons, rather than to Beowulf the Geat. Later in the poem Beowulf explains that although Heorogar, Hrothgar's elder brother, inherited the war-gear—and indeed the Danish throne, which it seems to symbolize—from their father Healfdene, he did not then pass it on to his son Heoroweard. Instead, Hrothgar came into possession of both war-gear and throne (see n. to p. 72). It is tempting to envisage Hrothgar's other nephew Hrothulf resentfully watching here as Hrothgar presents these symbolic heirlooms to Beowulf, and with them, perhaps, Hrothulf's own chance of succession—Wealhtheow certainly comes to understand that Hrothgar is planning to make Beowulf his heir (see n. to p. 40).

36 *He sang of Finn's troop . . . the Frisian slain*: see the Introduction for a fuller discussion of the story of Finnsburh and its relation to *The Fight at Finnsburh*. It is not clear from either of the two accounts (which themselves do not correspond in every detail) how or why the fighting began.

*Hildeburh, indeed . . . stricken with grief*: the poet's cryptic remark about Hildeburh and the honour of the Jutes could be understood in two ways: that she could not recommend their honour because they were treacherous would be a standard Old English understatement; on the other hand, if they did indeed behave honourably, fighting loyally for one side, then the resulting bloodshed was still a tragedy for Hildeburh. If, as seems likely (see n. to p. 37), there were Jutes on both sides of the conflict, there are a number of hypotheses one could formulate about their treachery, but because the episode is told so allusively in *Beowulf* it is impossible to work out the origins of the conflict.

37 *that Finn should . . . with the Jutes*: it is hard to believe that Finn would force the surviving Danes to share a hall with their opponents in the battle, so it has been argued that the poet is referring here to Jutes who fought with Hnæf and his men, perhaps including Hengest, who is now leading the Danes. This Jutish Hengest has been identified with the Hengistus whom Bede and other early historians name as one of the leaders of the Germanic tribes who arrived in England in AD 449. The tribes in question are said to be Angles, Saxons, and Jutes; the Jutes settle in Kent and Hengest is mentioned in the Kentish royal genealogy.

*although they . . . lordless men to do*: the clearest statements in Old English literature about the dishonour of serving the slayer of one's lord are in the *Anglo-Saxon Chronicle* entry for 755—commonly anthologized as 'Cynewulf and Cyneheard'—and in *The Battle of Maldon*. In both instances the retainers choose death in battle rather than that particular disgrace, and some scholars trace this sentiment back to what Tacitus says in his *Germania* about the behaviour of the Germanic tribes, though whether the *Germania* can usefully illuminate Old English literary traditions has been much disputed.

*images of boars*: see n. to p. 11.

*Then Hildeburh asked . . . Hnæf's pyre*: the especially close relationship in Germanic societies between a man and his sister's son is here poignantly reflected as Hnæf and Hildeburh's son are united in death on the same funeral pyre.

38 *The ravenous flames . . . finest men departed*: the flames of the funeral pyre which is the inevitable outcome of heroic conflict greedily swallow

warriors in terms very reminiscent of those in which Grendel is described devouring innocent Danes. The explicit moral is that the funeral pyre makes no distinction between Danes and Frisians; the implicit point is that warriors killed upholding heroic principles end up the same as those humiliatingly eaten by monsters.

*Then winter was over . . . the Jutes*: the lyrical description of spring bringing physical and spiritual release to the pent-up warriors is abruptly undercut; the coming of spring in fact precipitates the last bloody battle, for Hengest, having been incited by Hunlafing, now wants revenge more than freedom, and the better weather allows Danish reinforcements to help him put the revenge into practice.

39 *They sailed . . . her own people*: Hildeburh's return to Denmark—to 'her own people'—prefigures one of the poem's more shadowy allusions, the recapture of the Swedish king Ongentheow's elderly wife from Hæthcyn the Geat. Both women are victims of war, and Hildeburh's silence, especially following her bereavements, leaves unanswered the question of whether she herself felt her return to be a homecoming.

*Then Wealhtheow . . . in a feud*: the poet not only makes another ominous allusion to possible hostility between Hrothgar and Hrothulf, and to the murderous Unferth at the heart of Heorot, but also sets Wealhtheow's ceremonial entry in an unpropitious context.

40 *but leave this land . . . for you to die*: It is easy to understand Wealhtheow's careful corrective to Hrothgar's provocative generosity in offering to adopt Beowulf as his son, not only because she and Hrothgar have sons of their own who might expect to inherit, but also because Hrothgar's nephew Hrothulf might also be a contender for the throne. It is however hard to decide whether Hrothgar's offer to Beowulf is rash, or whether Hrothgar is long-headedly seeking to stabilize the situation by establishing Beowulf as a powerful future king. As we may infer from later Norse sources, the ensuing power-struggle in the next generation of Danes was indeed a bloody one (see n. to p. 72).

*I am convinced . . . when he was a boy*: again, Wealhtheow's anxiety may be detected here, as if she has a presentiment of what we—poet and audience—may suspect to be the case: that Hrothulf will turn against his uncle Hrothgar. Some critics, though, have preferred to see Wealhtheow as a confident, authoritative figure who wisely, rather than anxiously, sees the dangers of the situation and pointedly (even if fruitlessly) instructs the men on proper conduct. When Beowulf returns to Geatland, he faces a parallel situation: after Hygelac's death, he is offered the kingdom, but chooses to support Hygelac's young sons rather than rule himself, just as Wealhtheow obliquely recommends Hrothulf to do.

40 *the most handsome collar . . . a feud with the Frisians*: the glamour and grandeur of this necklace, especially in its association with the mythical Brosing necklace, in Norse tradition one of the goddess Freyja's treasures, is grimly undermined by the poet's allusion to its future: ransacked by unknown Frankish warriors when Hygelac is killed on a reckless raid. What becomes of treasure after the glorious ritual of its being given and received is one of the poem's darker themes. The story of Hama, who is alluded to in *Widsith*, is told in the Old Norse *Þiðreks saga*, in which a character called Heimir pits himself against Ermenaric but after twenty years enters a monastery—'chose long-lasting gain', as the *Beowulf*-poet says of Hama. His treasures and war-gear are bequeathed to the monastery, a sharply pointed contrast to the fate of the Danish necklace (see Garmonsway and Simpson, *Beowulf and its Analogues*).

41 *they had not tasted . . . take his rest*: this is another example of the poet's characteristic undermining of apparent peace, concord, and conviviality at Heorot.

43 *Many spirits . . . her son's death*: this brief resumé of Beowulf's victory over Grendel makes Grendel's mother's motivation—revenge—vividly clear. In much heroic literature, revenge is seen as a necessary and even laudable duty to one's kin; here we have a double distortion of the ideal: the avenger is monstrous rather than human, and female rather than male.

*The terror she caused . . . opposed to a man*: in the original, the poet claims that the terror Grendel's mother inspires is as much less as the terror a woman warrior inspires compared with that of a man in battle. This has often been seen as a curious lapse on the part of the author, since Beowulf's fight with Grendel's mother is considerably more terrifying and challenging than his victory over Grendel. But perhaps the poet's understatement is at work here: a female warrior might be taken as an awe-inspiring perversion of the norm—like an Amazon, in fact—so that the terror would indeed be greater rather than less.

45 *men do not know . . . mysterious spirits*: Grendel's unknown and unknowable immediate ancestry (to Hrothgar and the Danes, if not to the Christian poet) marks him off from human society—even Scyld, who arrives and departs so mysteriously, is the son of Scef (see n. to p. 2) and Hrothgar first identifies Beowulf as the son of Ecgtheow.

46 *These two live . . . the heavens weep*: this description of the home of Grendel and his mother bears a strong resemblance to St Paul's vision of Hell—the apocryphal *Visio Sancti Pauli*—which is recounted in an Anglo-Saxon sermon, Blickling Homily XVI. Exactly how the poem relates to these two versions of St Paul's vision has been debated, but influence from Christian conceptions of the topography of Hell is plain. (See Charles Wright, *The Irish Tradition in Old English Literature* (Cambridge, 1993).)

*Better each man . . . deeply mourn*: it is harder to accept this precept uncritically when we know that it is precisely the ethic which has motivated Grendel's mother.

*he who may . . . this world*: this sentiment is expressed very clearly in *The Seafarer*.

48 *in the morning . . . sail-road*: the association of sorrow and morningtime is conventional in Old English poetry, normally in connection with human misery being felt most acutely then. This is especially vividly expressed in *The Wanderer*.

50 *A full day elapsed . . . bottom of the lake*: critics have struggled with the improbability of Beowulf's descent lasting one whole day; some have translated 'a short time elapsed' in place of 'a full day'. But there is of course a basic implausibility in the idea of a fully armed and helmeted warrior swimming at all—and his opponent is in any case a creature of the imagination.

*some loathsome hall . . . could not touch him*: the monster fight in the analogous Old Norse *Grettir's saga* takes place in the damp cave behind a waterfall, a fully naturalistic setting which still requires a bold underwater swimming feat from the hero. But it is hard to say whether the (much later) *Grettir's saga* has rationalized the underwater hall in the poem, or whether the poet has imperfectly remembered a setting which the author of the saga has reproduced more clearly.

51 *for the first time . . . failed to live up to its name*: it has been argued that Unferth deliberately and maliciously lent Beowulf a defective sword, but the poet here seems to stress the sword's excellence hitherto.

52 *an invincible sword . . . quick of combat*: there are examples in Old Norse literature of supernatural creatures who can only be overcome by their own weapons—for example, the giant in *Hrólfs saga Gautrekssonar*—and in the Old Testament, David decapitates Goliath with Goliath's own sword (1 Samuel 17: 51).

53 *it seemed certain . . . the sea-wolf had destroyed him*: it is not clear why the Scyldings and the Geats should jump to the pessimistic conclusion that it is Beowulf's blood, rather than the monster's, which comes into view, but this is also a feature of the monster fight in *Grettir's saga*. Perhaps the pessimistic assumption simply emphasizes the magnitude of the hero's task, enhancing his success.

*the ninth hour came*: the ninth hour is about mid-afternoon. Since Christ died on the cross at the ninth hour, and the watching of the soldiers recalls the vigil at the Garden of Gethsemane, some critics have built a Beowulf/Christ allegory around these lines, with Grendel's mother's lair as an entrance to Hell, and the journey to and from its depths as a resurrection motif. The poet does seem to play with Christian topoi in a way which may seem strange or even tasteless to a modern reader: when he goes to fight the dragon, for instance, Beowulf has eleven companions.

53 *Then the battle-sword . . . the true Lord*: the bold juxtaposition of supernatural event—the corrosiveness of Grendel's blood melting the sword blade —and natural transformation—God's control over the seasons as when the ice of winter is melted in spring—is very striking here.

56 *On it was engraved . . . first been made*: the decoration of this ancestral sword depicts the history of the race of Cain, the phrase 'the origins of strife' perhaps referring to the killing of Abel by Cain, or the wickedness amongst men which provoked God to instigate the Flood. It was customary to engrave the name of the owner (or maker) on swords.

57 *Heremod . . . Scyldings*: see n. to p. 31 on Heremod. Ecgwala is not known elsewhere; it is possible to discern a faint parallel in the relationship between Heremod and the sons of Ecgwala on the one hand, and Hrothulf and the sons of Hrothgar on the other, but the allusion is not detailed enough to make any more of it.

59 *This land's grizzled guardian . . . many treasures*: this speech is commonly referred to by critics as 'Hrothgar's sermon'. Its wisdom—the advice of an old man to a younger hero—is a masterly example of the poet's ability to develop a set of ethics which is neither anachronistically Christian nor simply secular heroic. Its tone is, if anything, Boethian, especially in what is said about transience, pride, and foresight, and this is fitting given that Boethius himself was a Roman philosopher who was greatly admired by the Christian Middle Ages; *The Consolation of Philosophy* was translated by King Alfred the Great.

60 *the black raven gaily proclaimed sunrise*: widely throughout Old English and Old Norse literature, and even within *Beowulf* itself, the raven is a bird which feeds on corpses and thus often presages death in battle. The raven here, however, functions like a lark. Perhaps this deliberately reflects the radical transformation Beowulf has brought about for the Danes—or perhaps the ominous associations of the raven are still lurking in the image. That the Frankish warrior killed by Beowulf was called Dæghrefn ('day-raven') is a curious coincidence.

61 *Should Hrethric . . . warmly welcomed*: Beowulf's invitation to Hrethric may be more than simple hospitality; Beowulf may be delicately indicating that Hrethric will be welcome if he ever needs to take refuge with the Geats.

65 *Hygd, his queen . . . between the two seas*: Hygd is dramatically contrasted with Thryth, who, in feminist terms, violently repudiates the male gaze, but is then mysteriously tamed by her marriage to Offa. This Offa, the king of the continental Angles, is represented in Anglo-Saxon tradition as an ancestor of the eighth-century Offa of Mercia—one of the few links

with Anglo-Saxon England in the poem. The thirteenth-century English work *The Lives of the Two Offas* not only makes this connection but also tells the story of the once wicked Drida, whom Offa marries, but in fact fails to rehabilitate. (See Garmonsway and Simpson, *Beowulf and its Analogues*.) In Saxo's *History of the Danes* there is a similarly hazardous queen, Herminthruda; both Drida and -thruda are related in form to Thryth, although this is not an unusual element in Germanic names, and the woman who is dangerous to woo is a familiar folk-tale figure.

*Ongentheow's slayer*: Hygelac is (indirectly) the slayer of Ongentheow later in the poem, in the tangled history of the Swedish–Geatish feuds which form the background to Beowulf's reign in Geatland.

67 *peace-weaver*: the term may be applied metaphorically to any woman in Old English literature, but perhaps here we are to understand that Wealhtheow herself (whose name seems to mean 'foreign slave') has been married to Hrothgar as a pledge of peace—just as Freawaru is to be.

69 *A huge unearthly glove swung at his side*: the glove was not mentioned in the primary account of the fight with Grendel, although we need not expect that and Beowulf's resumé to be identical in every detail. It is odd, however, that the name of Grendel's first Geatish victim, Hondscio, which is also first mentioned in this passage, is a kenning for glove (literally, hand-shoe). In Old Norse mythology, the giant Skrymir has a huge glove—so monstrously big, in fact, that the god Thor and his companions rather comically camp out in it overnight.

70 *as the shadows lengthened . . . the call of the past*: Beowulf's version of the entertainment in Heorot may represent the impression it would make on a young hero; the poet offers his readers a poignant association of old age, elegy, and darkness.

72 *He, Heorogar . . . he loved him*: the fate of the next generation of Scylding cousins—Freawaru, Hrothgar's daughter; his sons Hrethric and Hrothmund; his nephews Hrothulf, the son of Halga, and Heoroweard, the son of his elder brother Heorogar—is ominously alluded to throughout the poem. We have heard Beowulf's plainly spoken prediction about Freawaru, and dark hints about Hrothulf's treachery—hints borne out by later Norse sources telling of the murder of Hroerekr (Hrethric) by Hrólfr (Hrothulf). These sources also relate the killing of Hrólfr/Hrothulf by Hjörvarðr, whose name is cognate with Heoroweard (see Garmonsway and Simpson, *Beowulf and its Analogues*). Such violence is a predictable outcome of the dynastic situation set out so clearly in *Beowulf*: Hrothgar has inherited his brother's throne, so that his sons, his nephews, and his son-in-law will all be contenders for the succession. It is not surprising that what must have been a notorious power-struggle is relatively well represented in Norse tradition; uniquely, *Beowulf* is set in the preceding

generation, at a time when the conflict is foreseeable, and apparently inescapable. Hrothgar's failed attempt to hand over the throne to Beowulf (see n. to p. 40) may be read as one of those dramatic moments which might have changed the course of history.

72 *Hygd wore that collar*: it is perhaps inconsistent that Hygelac was said earlier in the poem (see n. to p. 40) to have worn the necklet on a Frankish raid.

73 *He had been despised . . . glorious man*: the convention of the unexpected rise to eminence of an unpromising youth, familiar from fairy-tales as the triumph of the youngest or silliest son, is widespread in Germanic tradition.

*when Hygelac lay dead . . . Beowulf's hands*: it is often remarked that the poet moves with great rapidity over more than fifty years, but equally striking is his stark juxtaposition of Hygelac's prime, represented by the munificent treasure-giving in the hall, with his—and his sons'—violent deaths. The poet is concerned primarily with the contrasts of success and failure, endings and beginnings, death and life.

*a dragon began to terrify the Geats*: a dragon is a monster which belongs to Christian, classical, and Germanic tradition—an awe-inspiring and terrifying embodiment of evil.

75 *Hold now . . . this human race*: this elegiac passage—sometimes anthologized as 'The Lay of the Last Survivor'—is very similar in sentiment and verbal detail to other elegiac poems in the Old English tradition, notably *The Wanderer* and *The Seafarer*. The idealized picture of heroic life in the hall seems to represent the past—especially the heroic past—of the Anglo-Saxons as a whole. The interment of the gold is a vivid image of closure and finality, and here prefigures Beowulf's funeral at which gold is buried along with the hero—as useless to men henceforth as it was before it was mined. The 'Last Survivor''s invocation is very like a funeral oration. Structurally, this is another parallel to the image of the sparrow in the hall (see n. to p. 3): brightness bounded on both sides by unfathomable darkness. In Christian terms, there is also an echo of the parable of the talents (Matthew 25: 14–30); the gold is useless to the dragon, who finds it only to hoard it, while in flourishing human societies the gold is fruitfully used to develop and cement concord and loyalty in treasure-giving rituals.

76 *the wanderer carried . . . for a bond of peace*: the theft of the cup is a more complex act than at first appears: the thief steals it as a peace offering to his (unnamed) lord, which might be thought to mitigate the crime a little.

77 *his heart surged with dark fears*: this picture of an anxious, guilt-ridden Beowulf stands in contrast to his youthful certainty and confidence in Denmark.

78 *The eminent prince . . . life in this world*: foreshadowing Beowulf's death not only darkens the mood, but also increases the tension: the poet lets his audience know that a momentous event is about to take place.

*Then the giver of gold . . . vile mother*: the poet may here be suggesting that Beowulf is over-confident, and has underestimated his opponent.

79 *he declined . . . the Geats himself*: Beowulf's loyalty to the late Hygelac, and his admirable refusal to take advantage of his death by assuming the Geatish throne, contrasts with the internecine struggles of the generation of Scyldings after Hrothgar.

*Two exiles . . . gold-givers in Sweden*: the sons of Ohthere, Eanmund and Eadgils, in rebelling against their uncle Onela, offer another variation on the range of uncle/nephew relationships in the poem. Onela pursues his nephews to Geatland and kills Hygelac's son Heardred for harbouring them. The poet's allusive narrative technique means that we are never actually told that Onela killed his nephew Eanmund; we learn instead that Eadgils avenges his brother's death on Onela, with Beowulf's help.

81 *A death-bed . . . could not be requited*: the bereaved father, Hrethel, is powerless to act: he cannot avenge the death of one son by killing the other, and he cannot exact *wergild*—compensation for murder—from himself for himself. This accidental killing has an interesting parallel in Norse mythology: the god Baldr (whose name relates to Here*beald*) is unwittingly shot with an arrow by the blind god Höðr (whose name relates to *Hæth*cyn), and there is also an echo of the ancient Jewish tradition—widely taken up in medieval literature and iconography—that Cain was himself killed by an accidental shot from a blind descendant, Lamech, six generations later.

*In the same way . . . from the gallows*: Beowulf here imagines another dilemma of powerlessness, for a son who is executed as a criminal also cannot be avenged. The story of Hrethel's loss, and this hypothetical situation imagined by Beowulf, may mirror Beowulf's own dilemma: if he fails to rise to the dragon's challenge, he compromises his reputation as a hero and a leader of his people, and fails to protect them from the dragon; if he takes on the dragon he risks his life and thus the security of his kingdom.

83 *it was my battle-grip . . . silenced his heartbeat*: Beowulf's killing of Dæghrefn with his bare hands is an eerie echo of the fight with Grendel, when Beowulf refused to take advantage over his opponent by using weapons. It also bears out the literal meaning of Beowulf's name—bee-wolf, or bear—in its vivid evocation of Dæghrefn being crushed to death in Beowulf's savage grip.

86 *And Beowulf's companions . . . scared for their own lives*: although Beowulf is determined to take on the dragon alone, and instructs his men to watch from a distance, it seems to be expected that they will come to his aid if he gets into difficulties, rather than fleeing as cowards.

86 *his ancient sword . . . Ohthere's son*: the history of Wiglaf's sword recalls the feud between the Swedes and the Geats, when Eanmund and Eadgils rebelled against their uncle Onela and took refuge with Hygelac's son Heardred. As the poet (rather obliquely) explains in the lines following, Wiglaf's father Weohstan fought on Onela's side, and killed Eanmund for him; the sword in question was his reward. Since Beowulf later helped Eadgils in his revenge against Onela, it is ironic that Wiglaf uses the sword in his loyal support.

87 *It was Onela . . . brother's son*: that Onela rewards his nephew's killer is a grim variant on the uncle/nephew theme in the poem.

88 *I think . . . trappings of war*: Wiglaf's speech, apparently unheeded or even unheard by his companions, is very similar to the exhortations to courage and loyalty made in *The Battle of Maldon*.

93 *And let it be known . . . saltspray*: Beowulf's funeral mound provides an oblique echo to Scyld's ship burial: the final image is of the expanse of the waves, and the prospect of travelling great distances by sea.

*our family, the Wægmundings*: this is the first indication we have had that Beowulf is of Wægmunding stock.

94 *His slayer lay . . . cave-dragon*: it is sombrely fitting that the dragon as well as Beowulf should be killed in this momentous encounter. The power of a hero who faces an opponent so overwhelming that both are killed is evident also in Old Norse accounts of Ragnarök, the last battle of the gods, as Thor and the World Serpent fall together.

*No more did he fly . . . proud of his possessions*: the dragon is not the loathsome slithering creature of Old Norse tradition, but a magnificent flying beast which delights in its own grandeur.

97 *everyone remembers . . . in Ravenswood*: the poet has recounted earlier how the Geatish warrior Eofor killed Ongentheow, the old Swedish patriarch, in revenge for the killing of Hæthcyn. But here he delves even further back in time to the origins of the feud: Hæthcyn, it emerges, has attacked the Swedes first, and apparently abducted Ongentheow's queen—not, presumably, in order to force a marriage, for the queen is seen as a pathetic character, old, and humiliated by being stripped of her aristocratic jewellery. We now see the Geats as a belligerent, provocative tribe, and remember Hygelac's fatal, reckless attack on the Franks, who are ready to pay back the Geats as soon as an opportunity arises—as too, as the messenger predicts, are the Swedes.

*swore that . . . as sport for birds*: Norse sources characterize sacrifice to Odin as involving stabbing and hanging together, so that Ongentheow's savage taunts may indicate his intention to sacrifice the Geatish warriors.

98 *Then grey-haired Ongentheow . . . as Eofor willed it*: the battle at Ravenswood follows a familiar Germanic pattern of unexpected reversal, as the tables are turned on an apparently secure situation. Ongentheow triumphantly besieges the Geats, but finds himself ambushed when Hygelac arrives. Good examples of the pattern occur in the *Anglo-Saxon Chronicle* entry for 755 ('Cynewulf and Cyneheard'), in the Old English poem *Judith*, and in the Old Norse *Hrafnkels saga*. It is indeed just after the Danes and Geats have celebrated the demise of Grendel, and fallen into a complacent post-feasting sleep, that they are horribly surprised by Grendel's mother.

101 *lay under a curse*: the curse on the gold is mentioned rather late here; in Norse tradition, the treasure which Sigurðr recovered from the dragon was cursed, a motif powerfully elaborated in Wagner's Ring Cycle.

## THE FIGHT AT FINNSBURH

It is impossible to reconstruct with any clarity or certainty what may have preceded the opening of this fragment, but it seems likely that one of the warriors has been listing possible explanations for a light which has been glimpsed, the fragment beginning just as he gets to the third of them, and that Hnæf goes on to discount the suggestions in turn. The wider context seems to be one of a night attack on Hnæf and his men. These warriors are usually understood to be inside a hall (see n. to p. 106) although the dawn, a dragon, and hall-gables burning are all suggestive of a light seen outdoors, and from some distance away. Since the episode in *Beowulf* begins after Hnæf's death, it cannot be used to explain the events alluded to here.

106 *this enmity of people*: the enmity may be a reference to a feud between the two sides which has already been made clear.

*Sigeferth and Eaha . . . their footsteps*: the actions of the first four named warriors surely indicate that they (and Hengest) are defending a hall from the inside. Guthlaf is mentioned as a Danish warrior in the *Beowulf* episode; his companion there is Oslaf, whose name is probably a variant of Ordlaf here. The phrase 'Hengest himself' must indicate that Hengest has already been singled out as a figure of some significance amongst Hnæf's men.

*When he saw this . . . set upon his death*: if Sigeferth and his companions are indeed inside the hall, we must assume that Guthere and Garulf are part of the attacking force outside.

107 *Then the din of battle broke out in the hall*: confusingly, the impression given here is that the fighting takes place inside the hall, rather than in the doorway, as one might expect.

*Garulf, the son of Guthlaf*: Garulf is attacking the hall, and therefore presumably one of Finn's men; Guthlaf has already been mentioned as one of those inside the hall, defending. It may be that one of the memorable tragedies of the Finn story was that father and son found themselves on opposing sides; if there were indeed Jutes on both sides (see n. to p. 37) this would not be impossible. In the Old High German heroic lay *Hildebrandslied* father and son are ranged against one another in battle, and in the *Anglo-Saxon Chronicle* entry for 755 ('Cynewulf and Cyneheard') there are said to be relatives of the attackers amongst a troop of defenders. The poet of *The Battle of Maldon* points out that as well as a warrior called Godric who loyally fights to the bitter end, there was also a Godric who fled from the fight, but such coincidence of names is less likely in the present case given that the name Guthlaf only occurs in this one context.

107 *it seemed as if all Finnsburh were in flames*: both here, and in the reference to the gables burning, the dramatic image of a hall burning down (to be the fate of Heorot, according to the poet of *Beowulf*) is evoked.

*a wounded man . . . their wounds*: since Garulf, outside the hall, is said to be the first of many to fall, it is likely that this wounded man is one of those inside, who fought on for five days without loss. The guardian of the people who questions him would then be Hnæf, who is defending. But some scholars have taken 'guardian of the people' to refer to Finn, who would then be enquiring of one of his own front-line warriors how either the others in the vanguard, or the Danes inside the hall, were bearing up.

# WHO'S WHO

A glossary of proper names and place-names. (Entries in italics occur only in the *The Fight at Finnsburh*.)

**Abel** the brother murdered by Cain (see Genesis 4: 2)

**Ælfhere** a kinsman of Wiglaf

**Æschere** a retainer of Hrothgar who is carried off and killed by Grendel's mother

**Beanstan** the father of Breca, Beowulf's swimming opponent

**Beow** an early king of the Danes, the son of Scyld Scefing

**Beowulf** the hero of the poem. He is the son of Ecgtheow; his mother was King Hygelac's sister

**Breca** Beowulf's swimming opponent; a Bronding warrior

**Brondings** the tribe to which Beanstan and Breca belong

**Brosings** the owners or makers of the Brosing necklace, a legendary treasure (see n. to p. 40)

**Cain** the murderer of his brother Abel (see Genesis 4: 8), and in the poem, the ancestor of Grendel (see n. to p. 5)

**Dæghrefn** a Frankish warrior killed by Beowulf

**Danes** the inhabitants of Denmark. They are also referred to as Scyldings, Ring-Danes, Spear-Danes, and North-, East-, South-, and West-Danes

**Eadgils** a Swedish prince, son of Ohthere and brother of Eanmund, who seeks refuge at the court of Heardred of the Geats when exiled by his uncle Onela, and regains the Swedish throne with Beowulf's help

**Eagleness** a headland in Geatland where Beowulf dies fighting the dragon

*Eaha a Danish warrior*

**Eanmund** a Swedish prince, brother of Eadgils, killed by Weohstan, Wiglaf's father

**Ecglaf** the father of Unferth, the Danish warrior who taunts Beowulf

**Ecgtheow** Beowulf's father

**Ecgwala** a Danish king

**Eofor** a Geatish warrior who killed the Swedish king Ongentheow and was given Hygelac's daughter in marriage as a reward

**Eomer** the son of Offa, king of the Angles

**Ermenaric** a fourth-century Gothic king, known as a tyrant

**Finn** king of the Frisians

**Fitela** the nephew of Sigemund (see n. to p. 30)

**Folcwalda** the father of Finn

**Franks** enemies of the Geats (see map)

**Freawaru** the daughter of Hrothgar, to be married to Ingeld

**Frisia** the home of the Frisians, enemies of the Geats (see map)

**Froda** the father of Ingeld and king of the Heathobards

**Garmund** the father of Offa

*Garulf one of Finn's warriors*

**Geats** Beowulf's people, a tribe living in southern Sweden (see map)

**Gepidæ** a tribe related to the Goths, and originally based around the R. Vistula (see map)

**Grendel** the monster, descended from Cain, who terrorizes the Danes and is killed by Beowulf

*Guthere one of Finn's warriors*

**Guthlaf** a Danish warrior who fights at Finnsburh

**Hæreth** the father of Hygd, Hygelac's queen

**Hæthcyn** a Geatish prince who accidentally killed his brother Herebeald, and was himself killed by Ongentheow at the battle of Ravenswood

**Halga** a brother of Hrothgar

**Hama** the owner of the necklace of the Brosings

**Healfdene** king of the Danes, Hrothgar's father

**Heardred** the son of Hygelac and king of the Geats, killed by Onela after giving refuge to Eanmund and Eadgils

**Heathobards** the tribe to which Ingeld belongs (see map)

**Heatholaf** a Wylfing warrior killed by Beowulf's father

**Heathoreams** the tribe inhabiting the region in Norway where Breca is washed up after his swimming contest with Beowulf (see map)

**Helmings** the family of Wealhtheow, Hrothgar's queen

**Hemming** a kinsman of King Offa

**Hengest** the leader of the Danes after the death of Hnæf at Finnsburh; may be Jutish

**Heorogar** Hrothgar's elder brother

**Heorot** the great hall built by Hrothgar and raided by Grendel (see map)

**Heoroweard** Hrothgar's nephew, son of Heorogar

**Hercbeald** a son of Hrethel accidentally killed by his brother Hæthcyn

**Heremod** a king of the Danes before Scyld Scefing

**Hereric** Heardred's uncle, and perhaps Hygd's brother

**Hildeburh** Finn's wife, whose brother Hnæf and son are killed in the fighting at Finnsburh

**Hnæf** the leader of the Danes, killed in the fighting at Finnsburh

**Hoc** the father of Hildeburh and Hnæf

**Hondscio** a Geatish warrior devoured by Grendel

**Hrethel** king of the Geats and father of Hygelac; his daughter is Beowulf's mother

**Hrethric** a son of Hrothgar

**Hrothgar** king of the Danes and builder of Heorot

**Hrothmund** a son of Hrothgar

**Hrothulf** Hrothgar's nephew, a threat to Hrothgar's sons

**Hrunting** Unferth's sword, lent to Beowulf for the fight against Grendel's mother

**Hunlafing** a warrior of Hengest's who provokes him to revenge at Finnsburh

**Hygd** Hygelac's wife

**Hygelac** king of the Geats, Beowulf's uncle and lord

**Ing** early king of the Danes, perhaps mythical

**Ingeld** king of the Heathobards, to be married to Hrothgar's daughter Freawaru

**Jutes** a tribe involved in the fighting at Finnsburh (see map)

**Lapps** a tribe from northern Sweden and Norway

**Nægling** Beowulf's sword in the dragon fight

**Offa** fourth-century king of the continental Angles who married Thryth

**Ohthere** a son of the Swedish king Ongentheow

**Onela** the brother of Ohthere; exiles Ohthere's sons Eanmund and Eadgils, and kills Heardred for harbouring them in Geatland, but is himself killed by Eadgils, helped by Beowulf

**Ongentheow** king of the Swedes

*Ordlaf a Danish warrior*

**Oslaf** a Danish warrior (perhaps the same person as Ordlaf above)

**Ravenswood** site of a battle between the Geats and the Swedes

**Scyld Scefing** legendary founder of the Danish royal house

**Scyldings** the Danes (taking their name from Scyld Scefing)

*Secgan the people to which Sigeferth belongs*

*Sigeferth warrior of Hnæf*

**Sigemund** legendary dragon-slayer, a hero celebrated in Norse tradition (see n. to p. 30)

**Slaughter Hill** site of several battles between the Geats and the Swedes

**Swedes** enemies of the Geats

**Swerting** a Geatish warrior, uncle or grandfather of Hygelac

**Thryth** a cruel queen, unfavourably compared with Hygd, and 'tamed' by her marriage to Offa

**Unferth** a Danish warrior and retainer of Hrothgar who taunts Beowulf on his arrival at Heorot

**Vandals** the tribe to which Wulfgar belongs

**Wægmundings** the family to which Beowulf and Wiglaf belong

**Wæls** Sigemund's father

**Wealhtheow** Hrothgar's wife

**Weland** a legendary Germanic smith

**Weohstan** the father of Wiglaf

**Whaleness** Beowulf's burial place, overlooking the sea

**Wiglaf** Beowulf's kinsman and helper in his last fight

**Withergyld** a Heathobard warrior

**Wonred** a Geatish warrior

**Wulf** a Geatish warrior

**Wulfgar** a retainer of Hrothgar's who welcomes Beowulf to Heorot

**Wylfings** the tribe with whom Beowulf's father was in feud

**Yrmenlaf** Æschere's younger brother

**Yrse** Hrothgar's sister, married to the Swedish king Onela (see n. to p. 4)

**American Literature**

**British and Irish Literature**

**Children's Literature**

**Classics and Ancient Literature**

**Colonial Literature**

**Eastern Literature**

**European Literature**

**Gothic Literature**

**History**

**Medieval Literature**

**Oxford English Drama**

**Poetry**

**Philosophy**

**Politics**

**Religion**

**The Oxford Shakespeare**

A complete list of Oxford World's Classics, including Authors in Context, Oxford English Drama, and the Oxford Shakespeare, is available in the UK from the Marketing Services Department, Oxford University Press, Great Clarendon Street, Oxford OX2 6DP, or visit the website at www.oup.com/uk/worldsclassics.

In the USA, visit www.oup.com/us/owc for a complete title list.

Oxford World's Classics are available from all good bookshops. In case of difficulty, customers in the UK should contact Oxford University Press Bookshop, 116 High Street, Oxford OX1 4BR.

| | |
|---|---|
| JAMES BOSWELL | **Boswell's Life of Johnson** |
| FRANCES BURNEY | **Cecilia** |
| | **Evelina** |
| JOHN CLELAND | **Memoirs of a Woman of Pleasure** |
| DANIEL DEFOE | **A Journal of the Plague Year** |
| | **Moll Flanders** |
| | **Robinson Crusoe** |
| HENRY FIELDING | **Joseph Andrews** and **Shamela** |
| | **Tom Jones** |
| WILLIAM GODWIN | **Caleb Williams** |
| OLIVER GOLDSMITH | **The Vicar of Wakefield** |
| ELIZABETH INCHBALD | **A Simple Story** |
| SAMUEL JOHNSON | **The History of Rasselas** |
| ANN RADCLIFFE | **The Italian** |
| | **The Mysteries of Udolpho** |
| TOBIAS SMOLLETT | **The Adventures of Roderick Random** |
| | **The Expedition of Humphry Clinker** |
| LAURENCE STERNE | **The Life and Opinions of Tristram Shandy, Gentleman** |
| | **A Sentimental Journey** |
| JONATHAN SWIFT | **Gulliver's Travels** |
| | **A Tale of a Tub and Other Works** |
| HORACE WALPOLE | **The Castle of Otranto** |
| GILBERT WHITE | **The Natural History of Selborne** |
| MARY WOLLSTONECRAFT | **Mary** and **The Wrongs of Woman** |